THE MASTER AND THE SORCERESS
QUEENMAKERS SAGA VII

BY
BERNADETTE ROWLEY

THE MASTER AND THE SORCERESS
Bernadette Rowley
Copyright © 2020 Bernadette Rowley
All rights reserved.

First published 2017 by Bernadette Rowley
Second publication 2019 by Bernadette Rowley

ISBN: 978-0-6483105-0-1

Printing/manufacturing information for this book may be found on the last page

First Printing 2017 by Bernadette Rowley
Second Printing 2020 by Bernadette Rowley
2020 Cover Design by Dar Albert
Interior Design by
Business Communications Management bcm-online.com.au

VC:TMTS-20200715)

Acknowledgements

To Louise Cusack for her inspiration and advice over
the last twelve years.

To Duncan Carling-Rodgers for his assistance during the most
recent edits of The Master and the Sorceress and for the formatting.

To Dar Albert for her stunning covers

To my husband, Michael, and my sons for their unending love and
support and for sharing in the disappointments and
triumphs of a writing life.

Titles by
Bernadette Rowley

DEDICATION

Dedicated to my husband and three sons who lift me up
so I can fly free in my fantasy world of Thorius.

TABLE OF CONTENTS

CHAPTER 1

Kingdom of Thorius, the road between the King's seat of Wildecoast and the coastal town of Costa

KATRINE spurred her black stallion into a reckless gallop, the flinty coast road between Wildecoast and Costa disappearing beneath Demon's hooves. She was careless of the danger. There was little enough excitement in her life, and happiness was a condition she no longer recognized. Her gut clenched as it had on waking that morning and a familiar foreboding took its place. Nothing good would come of this day.

She had experienced such a warning on three past occasions. The first was the day Papa died, changing all their lives. The second time her sister's ship had sunk, almost taking Esta with it. The third was two days later when she had the joy of life seared from her in the Crystal Cave. She fingered the opal earring that was all they had recovered from the treasure hunt.

In disarming a magical trap, Kat had come close to death and the silver flecks in her blue irises were a legacy of the near disaster. Most days she wished she had died in that chamber. Death would be preferable to living each day in deep melancholy, waiting for a moment of happiness that might give her some respite.

Charging around a blind corner, Kat failed to see the man on the side of the road until she was almost upon him. He flung himself aside as she dragged on the reins. Demon wouldn't thank her tomorrow when his mouth was sore.

The man fixed her with a stormy grey gaze from the ditch he had landed in. *Oh, he is magnificent!* She tore her eyes away from his and allowed herself a leisurely exploration - from long dark hair tied in a ribbon at his nape to his olive complexion and the taut muscles of his bare chest and abdomen. Something dark and primitive passed between them, and then she remembered she shouldn't be staring.

"I'm sorry, but why are you stopped on a blind corner?" she asked, patting Demon's neck to soothe him.

* * *

James Tomel stared at the wild woman who had almost trampled him. She was stunning – her ebony tresses swirled in the fresh breeze, long muscular legs clad in black breeches gripped her horse, and piercing blue eyes speared him. He couldn't look away, as if a cord of senseless magic ensnared him. He shook his head. What had she said?

"Blind corner?" he snapped.

The woman dropped her eyes. Perhaps he had imagined the silver flecks prominent in her irises.

"It's nothing of the sort!" he said. "If you hadn't been galloping as though all the hounds of hell were after you there would have been plenty of time to avoid me." He pushed up from the ditch and brushed himself off, then grabbed his shirt from the cart.

The woman climbed down from her horse, scowling as if it were his fault.

"What were you doing, anyway?" She combed long violet nails through her hair. "Is there something wrong with your cart?" Her eyes, which so unnerved him, swept over the conveyance he used to dash between Wildecoast and Costa. It was a small cart pulled by a pony. It suited well when he needed to make a business trip and doubled as a racer at the Costa trap races, held four times a year.

"Not that it's any concern of yours, Madam, but I felt a wheel wobble and investigated." He shrugged into his shirt while the temptress crawled beneath the trap. James hurried to secure his pony so there was no movement while she was under the vehicle. She felt her way along the axle, inspecting the joins.

"Are you an expert in such matters?" he asked.

"I'm from a farm," she said. "I know my way around an axle."

She paused and the hairs stood up on his neck, a worm of unease wriggling in his belly. He shook it off as the woman emerged from under the cart and stood.

"I can't see anything that would cause a wobble, Sir, but I advise you to get the wheelwright to see to it when you reach town."

"Of course," he said, sarcastically "I would never have thought of that."

The sound of an approaching vehicle caught his attention. A fancy older coach appeared, the pair of chestnut horses pulling it breathing hard. "Seems everyone is forcing the pace today." He turned to the woman, surprised to see her chewing her lower lip. *Distracting…*

The coach stopped. The driver jumped down and strode up to them. "Lady Katrine!" he said. "You know how it worries me when you pull ahead like that!"

James stared, first at the red-faced coach driver and then at the raven-haired woman who stood, hands on hips, her expression a mix of defiance and regret.

"*Lady* Katrine?" Was this wild creature really a member of the aristocracy? He'd met no one like her. *And I would've remembered.*

She turned to him and the force of her smile punched his gut. "Lady Katrine Aranati," she said, shoving her right hand at him. "My friends call me Kat."

James took her smaller hand in his, not surprised to find calluses brushing his palm. A chill ran up his arm at her touch. "James Tomel, Master Jeweler, at your service, My Lady." He bowed.

"I'm pleased to meet you, Master Tomel." Her eyes dropped to his unbuttoned shirt and he released her hand to tidy himself up.

The driver cleared his throat. "Miss, I think we should be on our way, if you please. We'll lose light soon."

Lady Katrine nodded. "Yes, Mason, let's go."

Heat rippled through James as she again looked over his body.

"It was nice to make your acquaintance, Master Tomel." She strode to her mount and vaulted into the saddle. "I'm sorry for earlier."

"Wait! I'll ride with you. We're heading in the same direction and, with my trap in need of repair, it would be stupid of me to travel alone."

* * *

Kat smiled. James had no way of knowing she had used forbidden magic to mend the crack in his axle. She watched him tuck his shirt into his breeches, climb aboard his vehicle, and gather the reins. *Man, he is fine!* How did a craftsman stay so fit when he must spend day after day at his sedentary occupation? Her fingers itched to rake her nails over those stomach muscles; see if they were as hard as they appeared. Then she'd loosen the ribbon that restrained his dark hair and run her fingers through it. Kat realized both men were frowning at her while she sat unmoving on Demon.

She cleared her throat. "Yes, Master Tomel, of course you must travel with us." She clucked to her horse and set off with the coach by her side.

For the first half hour, Kat tried to focus on the countryside, ignoring the man trailing her coach in his small conveyance. She planned the task she had been sent to complete - that of moving Samael Delacost's parents to the Aranati estate. Eventually, however, James drew his vehicle alongside.

"Excuse me, Lady, but your name rings a bell. I've been trying to remember where I've heard it."

She tried to keep her expression bland. The whole of Wildecoast was still buzzing with the news of her sister, Esta, and her scandalous marriage to the pirate Delacost. Esta was expecting his child, due to deliver in four months. Kat tried to be joyful for Esta's sake, however, a baby would only make things worse when Sam returned to his thieving ways. True, he was trying to mend his life - the king had handed him over to Admiral Nikolas Cosara, who was Sam's half-brother, and responsible for keeping the pirate on the right side of the law. Yes, their family name was dirt right at this moment, and it was Esta's fault. She didn't wish to burden James with the sordid details.

"We're an old farming family," she said. "Our estate lies south of Wildecoast."

James frowned as if this shed no light upon his mystery.

Of course, it didn't! She turned to Mason. "How much longer until we reach Costa?"

Mason looked around at the landmarks. "About an hour, Lady Katrine. We'll be just in time to drop you at the Delacosts' and I can bed down the horses at the nearest inn."

Kat flinched. *He had to mention the Delacosts!*

James didn't appear to have heard. He was still riding, lost in his own thoughts, a frown on his handsome face.

I wonder if he likes to dance. She imagined being held in his arms and instinct told her he'd be her master in the dance and in life. *Where did that thought come from? I don't even like dancing!* She needed no man to order her life and keep her safe. A man would only clip her wings as Sam Delacost had done to Esta. She didn't seem to mind now, but she would when she was saddled with children while he roamed the oceans, free as the wind.

Kat picked up the pace a little and Mason went along with her. He must be keen to get to the inn. Perhaps he knew a serving girl there? She ground her teeth as James clucked to his pony and brought his rig up alongside again.

"Aranati, you said, My Lady?"

Kat glanced across at him and noted his grey eyes had turned flinty. *Oh no! He has made the connection!* "That's right, we farm crops, pigs, lambs, and cows. We've even bred horses from time to time. In fact, perhaps I'll try my hand at that again. I'm looking for a project!" She was rambling, she realized, and James scowled.

"I beg your pardon, My Lady," he said, "but there's no need for you to be so long- winded. I know exactly why your name is familiar now. Your sister destroyed my friend, Reid Vetta!"

A thousand big-winged moths battered at Kat's stomach as his words drove at her - not just the scandal then, but real damage to a loved friend. Kat knew Reid was devastated when, two weeks before their wedding, her sister ran off after Samael Delacost. However, her feelings on the matter were irrelevant; this was family and she must defend it.

"Yes, my sister is Esta Aranati and she was betrothed to Reid Vetta." Kat held her head high as she confessed.

"Do you have any concept of the damage your family has done to Reid?" Fury blazed from James's eyes and he drew himself up, appearing much larger than before. He stopped, forcing Kat to do the same. She swung her horse to face him.

"It must have been terrible," she said, "but in time he'll come to terms with his loss and be glad he never married a woman who didn't love him." To Kat's ears her words sounded unsympathetic, so how must they sound to James? *Damn Esta! Why isn't she here to defend herself instead of leaving me to explain her actions?*

"Oh, Lady! It's so easy to say those words. This is a man who lost his first wife *last year.*" James jumped down from his trap and paced as if the anger inside him needed a physical release. "Hasn't he suffered enough? He had convinced himself to try again, only to have your sister steal his heart then dump him two weeks later. And he injected funds into your estate which he'll never recover."

He stopped before her, the torrent of words dying, his fists opening and closing, shoulders hunched.

Kat dismounted, and Demon danced away from the angry man. James was a head taller than her and broad across the shoulders. Furious, he was more than a match for her. But she couldn't allow him to dominate.

"Esta tried to repay Reid, but he said he doesn't want reimbursement."

"He wants to be done with the whole sorry mess." James turned and strode to the side of the road and back. "Your sister has ruined his chances of a family. Do you think he'll ask another to become his wife after this debacle? He has thrown himself into his work, creating more amazing pieces than ever before, but who will enjoy the fruits of his labor?"

"Reid will work himself into an early grave," she breathed, imagining the master goldsmith alone and exhausted, afraid to sleep for fear of dreams of her sister.

"I won't allow him to do that," James said. "I'll lure him out of his workshop and persuade him there are better women than your sister in this world."

Kat's eyes snapped to his. "That's enough! You won't cast aspersions on Esta! She fell in love and followed her heart. I regret that Reid was hurt, however the alternative would've been much worse."

"Love! Reid *loved* your sister. She would've been happy as his wife. He would've given her everything."

"Esta might have been content for a while." So much had been happening back then, she reflected. Esta had lost her ship and almost her life, the estate finances were exhausted, and Kat had faced a crisis of her own - still faced it. She didn't blame Esta for not knowing which way to turn. "But, in time, she would've resented her marriage of convenience and then Reid would've paid dearly."

"You don't know that," James said, hands on hips.

"There's no happiness in a loveless marriage."

He threw up his hands. "Why am I arguing with you? You'll always defend her. Let's just say I'm getting an interesting insight into the morals that exist in your clan."

Kat put all her strength and frustration into the slap, leaving a bright red handprint on his cheek.

"How dare you?" she spat. "You know nothing, *nothing* of me *or* my family. If I never see you again it will be too soon." She shoved him out of the way and mounted Demon. Digging her heels in, she went from standing to a gallop in seconds, leaving her coach behind once more.

CHAPTER 2

JAMES'S cheek still throbbed with the sting of Lady Katrine's hand as he passed the outer wall of the small town of Costa - his home. He had left the road and taken a longer route soon after the altercation with Katrine, having no desire to exchange any more words nor receive more clouts. She packed a wallop but, now he had cooled down, James regretted his angry words. It was unfair to tar the feisty young woman with the same brush as her sister. If he ever saw her again, he'd apologize. However, he wouldn't apologize for defending his friend.

He sighed. It would be good to get home and enjoy the luxury of familiar surrounds and food. He hated being on the road, not knowing what was around the next corner or whom. He grimaced as he recalled Katrine and the effect she had on him. She was the opposite of everything he normally found attractive in a woman. She didn't even wear skirts! However, there was something about her wild ways and striking eyes that would make it difficult to forget her. And now he knew she was related to the woman who had hurt Reid, there was less chance he could stop thinking about her.

He pulled up at his mansion. The manager came from the stables to take the pony and rig away.

"I trust you had a good trip, Master Tomel?"

"Not bad, Micc," James said, "but I'm glad to be home."

"Mistress Lary has supper prepared. We hoped you might return today."

"Any news?"

Micc stopped and turned back. "Damned dark elves are causing trouble again to the west. Not many but enough to be a nuisance. I've increased patrols of your properties and the town watch has beefed up its numbers - not sure where they got the coin for it. They've no money for anything else in Costa." He stomped away, grumbling to himself, and disappeared around the corner of the mansion.

James hefted his bag and sword, and entered the house to be greeted by Mistress Lary, his house keeper. She was a woman in her middle years and married to one of the town guards; hence, she returned to her own home in the evenings. James was glad to have the place to himself at night especially with the hours he kept when working on a project.

Pushing all thoughts of women from his mind, James entered his room to find his maid, Eva, her belly round with child, in the process of lugging in hot water for his bath.

"I've told you, Eva," he said, taking the pail from her and pouring it into the tub, "this work is too heavy for you. Get someone to help."

"It's lighter and safer than my job at the inn." She smiled and took the empty pail from him, then turned and left.

James stripped off his dusty clothes, mulling over the changes needed once Eva had her child. She could no longer live in the tack room which had been hastily cleared out to provide a home for her. Once the baby came, Eva would need a room in the house. James sighed as he imagined the changes a newborn would bring.

Naked, he stepped into the tub which was only half-full of hot water. Before he had a moment to himself, Dant, the strapping young stable hand and general help, carried in two more pails of hot water and added them to the tub.

"I see Eva managed to find someone to help with the bath," James said. "I'd consider it a favor if you could assist with her heavier chores, Dant."

"Right you are, Master." Dant grinned. "You did a good deed bringing Eva here."

"I couldn't leave her there." James lathered his arms as he remembered the day he walked into his local and saw one of the serving girls was pregnant. He had taken Eva with him and found a new inn to patronize. It still shocked him to learn the innkeeper had been running a brothel on the side and that his girls worked on their backs as well as their feet. Eva was only eighteen summers old! "Only I didn't realize she had no parents."

"Got more than you bargained for that day, Master," Dant said, his lazy grin lighting his odd-colored eyes - one blue and the other green.

James smiled. "It has all worked out for the best, but I need you to watch out for her, make sure she looks after herself and the babe. I'll make enquiries about a midwife next week."

"Right you are, Master." Dant bobbed his head as he left James to his bath.

He was lucky in so many ways. His staff were loyal even if he had the knack of bringing home strays. All of them had a tale of woe to tell which led them to him. Perhaps it was why they were so loyal - he had given them work or shelter when they fell on hard times. James had known privilege as a youngster, and he was driven to pay forward his good fortune to the people who worked for him. In return, all he wanted was a quiet life of order and peace.

He mused on his desire for order in his life. His parents had mapped out his existence from birth. They'd been sure he would willingly inherit the family farm and raise sheep and beef cattle. James wanted nothing of the sort. Every trip to the king's seat at Wildecoast exposed him to the jewelry worn by members of the court. He had longed to make pieces the aristocracy could pass down to their heirs. Perhaps it was a strange life for a farmer boy, but he was happy working with his gold, silver and gemstones. And Mother and Father had six other sons to work the farm.

The chaotic life on the farm was another reason for James's love of order. Seven sons born within ten years meant his six younger siblings had tried to best him at everything from riding to fighting and wrestling steers. Whenever he obtained anything of value, it was more than likely to disappear, only to end up in a younger brother's possession. Nothing was his and everything was shared, including his bedroom, until he left at age seventeen. It was then his life really started - when he was apprenticed to a master jeweler.

Master Anza had been a breath of fresh air. He welcomed James into his home and business, giving him a room of his own and tools to work with. In many ways, James was the son Anza never had. His four-year apprenticeship was completed in two, but James had stayed on, perfecting his craft and stunning his teacher with the brilliance of his designs. He could have remained with the older man, but, at the end of four years, he was eager to branch out on his own.

James had a hankering to move south and he chose the small seaside town of Costa. The commissions earned by making pieces for several of the Wildecoast ladies enabled him to purchase a small mansion, and his wealth and fame grew. He had designed an unusual chain mail choker for Queen Adriana and, since then, had been too busy to accept all the requests made by eager nobility. Perhaps it was time to enlist the help of an apprentice? Each time James had this thought, he shuddered at the idea of someone disturbing the tranquility of his workplace.

And speaking of tranquility, it was luxury to be in his own room, relaxing in his bath. The difficulties of his trip home faded as James lay back in the perfectly warm water and smiled.

* * *

Kat had been greeted with warmth by Samael's parents, which was a balm to her jangled nerves. She couldn't shake the shame and anger James's words caused. Harah and Claus drew her in, and she was soon ensconced by the fire with a blanket and a mug of tea. They rarely looked her in the eyes but had many questions of her trip, her sister and their son.

"We cannot wait to be grandparents," Harah said, mopping a tear from the corner of her eye. "Esta is a fine young woman and just the one to tame our Samael. We had despaired, and worried we would lose him. Now I think all will be well." The older woman beamed as though truly content.

Oh, to be so happy! It was on the tip of her tongue to remind Harah that Sam still went to sea on dangerous missions, but she thought better of it. *Let her have her happiness.*

"He certainly is transformed, Mistress Harah." Kat was at a loss to think of anything else to say. She must keep her objections to the union private. She was here to help them move and anything else was none of her business.

Claus topped up her mug and offered another biscuit. "Tell us of the estate and where we shall live, Lady Katrine," he said. "I find myself looking forward to being busy again."

Kat smiled. "There is much to do, Master Delacost. You only need to tell Esta what projects you wish to take on. She's excited to be welcoming you soon, and sorry not to be able to travel here herself."

Harah waved her hands. "There is nothing to be sorry for. She is with child. We'd be angry if she put herself and the babe at risk. We'll see her soon enough."

"You're kind," Kat said. "I admit I was fearful she'd insist on coming. She is usually so bossy." Kat fell silent, wondering if Esta was feeling as well as she said she was.

Harah grinned. "Their babe will be a handful. I can't wait to see him or her."

Kat remembered the earlier question. "Our estate is a day's travel south of Wildecoast. We grow or make almost everything we need, and, until Sam came along, things were tough. His money has meant we can pay our staff and plant new crops. We've been able to repair the fences around the cattle pastures." She paused to look at Claus. "There are so many buildings in need of repair, you have years of work ahead of you."

He positively glowed in response to the news. Kat smiled back at him. He and Harah would be good company for her mother who was often lonely. She hoped they all got along.

"Mother has insisted you stay in the main house until we can have accommodation built for you. Perhaps you'd like to help with that as your first task?"

Harah frowned. "Will we not be in the way? Two extra old folk around the house?"

"It's a large house, with plenty of room. Mother is preparing her best guest room as we speak. It's getting a whitewash and we've commissioned my Aunt Paurella, the queen's dressmaker, to replace the drapes and bed covers. You'll be quite comfortable."

Harah clasped her hands over her bosom. "I can hardly believe this is happening. For so many years we wondered if Samael would go away to sea and not return. We worried ourselves sick. And now he will give us a home, a family, *and* a grandchild."

Claus clasped his wife's hands. "You can believe, my dear. Our faith in that little babe thirty odd years ago has been rewarded. We took him in when Vitavia couldn't look after him and now he has given us all this."

Tears sprang to Kat's eyes as she listened to the pair. They deserved this chance at a new life after decades of struggle. She couldn't help wondering if she deserved hers too. Kat cleared her throat and stood, placing the mug carefully on the hearth.

"I'll settle into my room and then I must begin the task I was sent here for."

Claus stood too. "Rest for the night, my dear. It's late and you're tired."

"Yes," Harah said. "Unpack and then please join us for the evening meal. It's almost ready."

Kat nodded and hurried from the room, uncomfortable in their presence. She felt like an outsider in their home and their lives, but it would be better when she got to know them. She closed the door of her room and rested against it, eyes closed. How could she haul herself out of this abyss she had fallen into?

CHAPTER 3

THE next morning dawned fine and bright. Kat was up early, imbued with enthusiasm after a good night's sleep. For once the nightmares that had dogged her since the Crystal Cave stayed away. Perhaps it was sheer exhaustion that caused the break in her usual nightly routine.

She made her bed, though she never would at home. Mother had always taught Kat and her sister to be good guests, and tidying after oneself was part of that. Kat joined Harah in the kitchen and her hostess promptly placed a warm bowl of oats before her. *Porridge!* Kat barely managed not to grimace.

"Thank you, Mistress Delacost," she said, ladling honey and milk over the mixture as well as a decent measure of dried fruit.

"I always say a good breakfast sets you up for the day." Harah bustled back to the fire where she was preparing a loaf for the oven. "And please call me Harah. We are to be family!"

"Thank you, Harah. Mother says the same." Kat smiled, though a good breakfast on the farm consisted of bacon and eggs with sausages, mushrooms and fresh bread. She spooned the porridge into her mouth, determined to finish it. "Where would you have me start with the packing?"

Harah turned from placing the bread in the oven. "I'll begin with the kitchen, but I need more trunks I can pack into." She pulled out a gold coin, examined it and offered it to Kat. "Would you take this coin and purchase three large trunks from the marketplace?"

Kat took the offered coin. "It will buy much more than three trunks, Harah."

"Acquire anything else you think might be necessary, my dear. I need a new broom and perhaps a pail for water." She sounded distracted. "Now, where did I put the pan?"

Kat smiled. "I can see you're busy, so I'll be going. I may be most of the morning as I need to stop by the inn and collect the coach." Harah waved at her, and Kat left the kitchen. She returned to her room to retrieve her coat and left with a wave to Claus who was whitewashing the outside of the cottage.

She decided to walk to the inn and, as she did so, she wondered if she'd need to find Mason or if she could simply walk into the stables and hitch the team to her coach. Dressed as she was, in breeches and tunic, she doubted it. Someone would take her for a thief, and she'd find herself in trouble. She ground her teeth at the need to rely on Mason, but it was the sensible thing to do. Did this mean she was becoming responsible, growing up? At twenty-four, she supposed it was high time.

She stepped into the common room of The King's Crown and looked for her driver. There were few patrons at this early hour of the morning, and those present were eating their breakfast. She spotted Mason chatting to a serving girl over by the hearth and joined him. The girl bobbed a curtsy and walked away.

"Morning, Miss Katrine," he said, climbing to his feet. "I was about to come find you."

"Well, I've found you instead. Mistress Delacost has sent me into town to shop and I need the coach."

"Right away," he said, leaving his unfinished meal and throwing down a few coins. He led the way out the back to the stables.

Kat received a lot of interest as she waited for Mason to hitch the team to the coach. She would've helped, but it would've attracted more notice. She chewed her lip, wondering if she should have donned a gown to go shopping. The last thing she wanted was men ogling her backside in the tight breeches that were her favored garment. She wished her coat was a shade longer. A tendril of anger wormed its way up from her gut. Why should she have to worry about such a thing? Men didn't have to.

One of the stable hands eyed her with unconcealed lust. As he made to approach her, she bent down and pulled a knife out of her boot, testing the edge with her thumb. Out of the corner of her eye, she saw the man back up and disappear into a nearby stall. Two others laughed nervously. Kat ground her teeth. She was more than capable of defending herself, but she didn't wish to prove so. She hoped the man and his friends wouldn't seek to test her knife skills.

Shaking her head, she hopped up beside Mason. They rolled out of the stable yard and took the wide cobbled road toward the market. Mason kept up a monologue about his experiences at the inn last evening, so she only had to nod and murmur. It suited her as her mind was on other things. Now she was in Costa, she was impatient to get the task of moving the Delacosts done and get home. She'd rather not run into grumpy James Tomel, and, the longer she lingered, the greater the chance of coming face to face with him again. The thought of his accusations made her palm itch. He had no right to assume and none to judge either.

They arrived in the market square, and Kat had all her purchases made within the hour. The urgency she had arrived with melted away and she enjoyed browsing the stalls, all with such varied wares - from fish, fruit, and vegetables to pies and bolts of cloth from all over the kingdom. She was eager to discover where each item came from and lingered to chat with several merchants. As long as she kept on the move, she didn't attract much attention.

"Miss, I think we should return with our purchases," Mason said, as she paused in front of a stall displaying silver bangles. She had searched for a bangle with a wolf's head on it for ages.

"You go back, Mason," she said, examining each trinket. "I'll be fine by myself."

"You should come with me," he said. "There's plenty of weird folk here."

"Then I'll fit right in." She fixed the driver with a bright smile.

"Your sister wouldn't want me to leave you."

"My sister will never know if you don't tell her." Kat cast Mason a stern look, usually enough to close any argument.

"Well," he said, "if you're sure."

"Go and deliver the goods to Harah and Claus, then you can have a break. I'll meet you back at the house for the heavy lifting midafternoon."

"Right you are, take care."

He slipped away through the crowd, and Kat forgot about him as soon as he was out of sight. Why did men think you were only safe when they were around? She had traveled by herself before, through more danger than this market provided. A shiver went up her spine at the thought. She surveyed her surroundings for the source of the threat.

A scrawny man in dirty rags slunk through the crowd at the stall across from the jewelry stand, and, as she watched, he stopped behind a farm wife wearing a straw hat. His hand slipped into the bag the woman carried over her shoulder.

Without thinking, Kat sent a sliver of magic shooting toward the thief who shrieked at the top of his lungs, snatched his hand back, and ran for his life. She smiled to herself. *That will teach him to steal from hard-working farmers!* A growl sounded off to her right, and she turned to see what made the noise.

Only ten yards away, a huge grey dog stood, its malevolent yellow stare fixed upon her, lips curled in a snarl. Dread exploded in her heart as she recognized deadly intent in its eyes. *Run!*

Kat burst out of the crowd in front of the stall and charged up the street, her boots snapping against the cobbles. Rapid pad falls and snarling followed. Whatever the thing was, it wouldn't give up easily. She cast a look back. The dog from hell had gained on her in that short time. Snapping her head to the front, she looked about for some sort of rescue, but the appearance of the beast had sent market patrons flying into alleys and under stalls. The road before her was almost deserted.

Her breath burned in her lungs and blood pounded in her ears. Desperation made her clumsy, and she stumbled, clutching at a post at the side of the road. There was a shop! She lunged for the door, shoved it open, and slammed it shut behind her. The huge body of the dog crashed against the door with a force that shook the whole front of the premises. Growling and high-pitched yowling echoed through the building. Keeping her back to the door, she surveyed her surroundings for the first time.

"You!" she said, the man before her enough to distract her from the dog outside.

"What the deuce are you doing here, Lady?" James Tomel wiped his hands on an apron and walked toward her, eyes stormy and dark hair spilling from its bindings. "And what's that damned awful noise? It sounds like all the hounds of hell are outside my shop."

"*Your* shop?"

"Yes, and I'll have you know I don't need you bringing trouble to my door."

The door banged against her as the creature slammed into it again. "Well, I'm sorry," she said, gritting her teeth to stop them chattering. "It was that or let it eat me."

He blinked. "What do you mean?"

"That beast out there is huge! I was shopping in the market, and the next thing it's chasing me as though I'm its next meal. What are we going to do?"

James frowned, then squared his shoulders as the door shuddered again. "I have a back door. I'll grab my knives and move around to the front of the shop, then dispatch it."

She must be hearing things. "You're a tradesman. You can't go around killing dangerous dogs. You're not trained for it!" Her voice rose so high she didn't recognize it. *Damn it!* She had never been one for hysterics, but her hands shook so hard she knew she couldn't have picked up a knife, let alone thrown it.

James sent her a contemptuous look. "And you know me so well." He walked back behind the counter and collected five knives, two of which he slipped into his boots, then pulled on a chest holster where he stowed another two. One knife in hand, he stalked out the back.

"Wait! James!" She abandoned the door and followed the jeweler, catching up to him as he opened the back door. "I'm coming with you."

His eyes bugged. "Stay here. Bad enough you brought me this menace. I don't want you getting in my way."

She watched him walk away, irritation showing in every ounce of his body. But she couldn't let him face the thing alone with only five knives to defend himself. And she couldn't use her magic in public, not to the extent she would need to vanquish that dog anyway. Her knives would be as useless as James's. She cast her eye up and down the alley and spotted a broom with a thick handle lying against the wall. It would have to do. She seized her weapon and followed James around the corner of the shop to the street.

Kat poked her head around the side of the building just as James whistled at the beast. Her eyes darted to the hound as it turned to face the intruder. The dog launched itself toward James who braced himself, feet apart and knives at the ready. She charged into the street, brandishing the broom, and came to a halt beside James. The dog slid to a stop, its gaze shifting between the two humans.

"What are you doing?" James hissed from the corner of his mouth.

"Saving your behind. Knives are too slow. You'd be fortunate to get one thrown before he was upon you."

The dog studied them, perhaps wondering if two humans might be overcome as easily as one. Kat kept her eyes on it, noting the heavy jaw and muscled shoulders. If she could get the broom end in its jaws, perhaps James had a chance with his knives. At that thought, James's first knife hurtled at the beast, lodging in its shoulder. It screamed in pain and spun to bite at the blade. James seized the chance to hurl another knife at its exposed flank. The second one hit its target too.

"Nice throwing," she said, not taking her eyes from the howling creature. Before James had time to throw again, the dog turned and lunged at them, its movements awkward. Blood sprayed across the cobblestones. Kat jabbed with the straw end of the broom and the beast snapped at it, seizing the bristles and shaking his head from side to side whilst still moving forward. She was pushed backward, frantically trying to stay on her feet. Her heart pounded, breath straining in her chest. The movement of the beast stabbed splinters into her palms and fingers.

Another two of James's blades appeared in the left ribcage of the dog but Kat hardly noticed as she fought to keep the creature on the end of her broom. Blood poured from it, and it showed signs of weakening. Would its demise come soon enough? Or should she risk using her magic?

The beast surged forward and caught her by surprise. Her hands slipped off the handle and it was upon her, its weight bearing her to the cobblestones. Her skull cracked on stones and pain blasted through her head. With her last shred of desperate strength, she managed to get her hands around the dog's neck. Its yellow fangs were mere inches from her face, and she retched at the stench of its breath. Her arms trembled with the effort of holding it back. It wouldn't be much longer - already the threat of those teeth inched closer to her throat. She tried to gather her magic, but as she did, her hands relaxed their grip on the beast's neck. She screamed, fear, anger, and frustration battling for supremacy. And then the pressure on her arms ceased as the dog collapsed onto her chest.

Kat flung her arms out to the side, tears streaming as she drew great gasping breaths into her tortured chest. *I'm safe!* The weight lifted from her as James grasped the beast by the scruff of the neck and hauled it away. She rolled to her side and sobbed, tears mixing with the blood from the fearsome hound.

"Are you whole, Katrine?" James clasped her shoulder and his gentle finger probed the back of her head. "You're bleeding."

"I'm alive, that's all I care about." She dried her eyes on the crisp white handkerchief he offered and climbed to her feet with his help. The world tilted and she grabbed his shoulders, eyes closed to stop the spinning.

"You were foolish to intervene."

His voice soothed though he admonished her. *Strange.* She opened her eyes and met his serious gray gaze. *Serious and frightened!* Perhaps he did care a little what befell her. "I'm steady now." As she slipped her hands from his shoulders, he released her waist but stayed near. She looked down at the dog and knelt to examine it. A wave of sorrow brought fresh tears and she brushed them away. *Why should I feel any regret for the loss of this creature that was trying to kill me?*

"Come into the shop," James said. "I need to clean your head wound."

"In a moment." Kat hardly heard him. She pushed her grief aside and tried to concentrate on the body. The beast was the size of a wolf, with short grey hair, heavy snout, and stumpy ears. Its eyes were red but what drew her attention were the feet. There were six toes on each paw and the back feet had retractable cat-like claws that were huge and razor sharp. *Ideal for disemboweling prey.*

She shuddered and exposed the claws for James to see. "I wouldn't have lasted long had it not been almost dead when it leaped on me." She stood, walked over to a bench near the wall of the shop, and sat. Townsfolk surrounded the beast, poking at it with their boots and muttering. Kat kept her eyes down lest they blame her for its presence.

James spoke to a stout old man wearing a watch on a gold chain, then joined her on the bench. "The mayor says they haven't seen a night hound in these parts for fifty years."

Her gut clenched. "They're legend only. Used to scare children into staying close to home."

"He took one look at the hind paws and declared it a night hound. I want to know more."

"What will they do with it?"

"He wants to study it, then it will be burned."

She shuddered. "I never want to see that thing again." She thought back to what she was doing before the dog attacked. *Witchcraft.* Had the thing been attracted to her magic? It was said the hounds served the powers of darkness so it seemed likely they might be able to detect her sorcery. She shuddered again. If the hound was attracted to her spell, why had this never happened before? There must be another explanation.

James was talking. "…get you inside before the watch comes asking questions. You're in no condition for it." He helped her up and into the shop then seated her near his wash basin.

As he bathed her wound, he kept up a soothing run of useless conversation. "It's only a small injury, but you've lost some blood and taken a knock to the head. You'll have a headache. I'll fix a powder for you and you must rest on the pallet I use when I stay here overnight. Then I'll take you home."

The fear and tension drained from Kat as she closed her eyes and let his voice wash over her.

Kat woke with a start. She was on a pallet on the floor and a lamp bathed her in its gentle golden light. *Where am I?* She surged up and pain smashed through her skull.

"Ahh!" She grasped her head and battled a wave of nausea.

"Lie back before you pass out," James said, his hand a gentle pressure on her shoulder.

She did as she was told, and the pain subsided to a thudding ache in the back of her skull. "What time is it? I must get back to the Delacosts and Mason. They'll be worried."

"Never fear. I sent a message to them. Mason is bringing your coach."

"Oh…" She experienced an unreasonable pang that James wouldn't see her home himself, then cursed herself for a weak and feeble woman. *I'm not weak! I saved James, not the other way around.* "You've been kind, James, and I thank you."

"Your man should be here soon." He reached behind him and produced a silver goblet. "I've mixed this powder for your headache." The liquid in the cup was bitter, but she drank it all down and ate the bread he provided.

"This is excellent bread," she said. "Your wife's?"

"I'm not married. My housekeeper baked this." His words were stilted as though he would rather not talk about his private life.

Her heart leaped at the revelation of James's single status, but she reined it in. No point going silly over the man. It was a passing attraction they shared, or, rather, that *she* felt. She had no idea if James sensed it too. He had already told her what he thought of Kat and her kin.

"Look," he said, sliding his hand through his hair. "I was rude yesterday. It was unfair to blame you for what happened to Reid. I apologize."

She stared at him, and he looked right back as if her eyes were as normal as anyone's. "You don't have to apologize just because I'm hurt or because I saved your life."

His mouth fell open. "I… you…*you* saved *my* life? I was perfectly capable of handling that pup on my own!"

"Huh, there was no evidence of it when I arrived. Do you really believe your knives would have stopped a full charge? You did see those claws on the hind feet, did you not? We would've been picking up your entrails for days!"

"I had it covered," he said, through gritted teeth.

"Well, Sir, you may think what you wish, but it was my arrival which gave the dog pause and allowed you time to get your knives into it."

He scowled at her, the muscles of his jaw tensing and relaxing. Finally, he looked at the ceiling. "I admit you handled yourself well. There's no point fighting over who saved who. And I apologized because I was rude, not for any other reason."

She nodded. "Then I accept. Reid must be a good friend."

"He's a true and decent man, but if I speak of it again, I'll only be angry, so let's change the subject."

"My sister is a good person, James."

"You must say that because you can't believe anything else." He stood and walked away, his fingers again coursing through his shoulder length locks. The band that usually restrained them had long since fallen out. She admired his broad shoulders and again experienced an itch to run her fingers through his hair. It must be the head injury putting such insane fancies into her mind. The man disliked her. Besides, there was no room for romance in her life. How could she inflict her deep melancholy on another being? She must find a way to live with herself before contemplating a partner.

Kat sat up, waited for the room to stop swaying, and then stood. "You're wrong, you know. I'm not blind to my sister's shortcomings."

He turned to face her. She must have looked a sight because he hurried across and clasped her forearm. "I'm not sure you should be on your feet."

She shook her head and immediately wished she hadn't as the queasy feeling struck her stomach. "I'm trying to explain. Stop changing the subject."

"It doesn't matter." His fingers tightened on her flesh. "I've apologized for my treatment of you, so let that be the end."

She let out a huff of annoyance. "You're so stubborn. I can't stand to be in your presence a moment longer." She twisted out of his grip and tottered toward the door. "I'll wait outside." At least there she wouldn't be confronted with his virile strength, his taunting, musky male smell, and his overbearing attitude.

"Katrine." The word was filled with regret and frustration.

She stopped but kept her back to him. What was this that swirled between them? Her name on his lips seemed to whisper that he was affected by her. Or was she delusional?

"I'm sorry," he said, "I don't know what else to say. Please stay inside until your carriage arrives. There may be more night hounds out there."

Kat swallowed a sudden burst of fear and turned to face him. She didn't lower her eyes, just let him see who she was - a woman changed in a crystal chamber, by magic. A woman alone. And she knew he cared about her, if only a little.

She said nothing, but sank into a nearby chair and closed her eyes.

CHAPTER 4

JAMES handed the reins of his horse to a groom and entered his mansion, slamming the door behind him. He was late for supper, but it would have to wait. He needed to change his clothes and have a wash. The blood of the night hound had lodged in his nostrils along with the perfume of a certain feisty woman. His housekeeper came to greet him. He threw up his hand to silence her and kept walking to his bedroom. *Alone. I need to be alone.*

His usual bath was prepared. He stripped off his clothes and stepped into it, sliding under the water until he was completely submerged. His thoughts leaped to the events of the day - Katrine bringing the night hound to his door, her willingness to place herself in danger for him, and the revelations of their connection. He'd ignore the attraction, of course. He had his life planned out, and it definitely didn't include Lady Katrine Aranati. *Imagine Reid's face if I told him of a relationship with the sister of his former fiancée.* He'd be furious. Well, it would never happen.

Of equal concern was the appearance of the night hound - a creature out of legend. What had brought it to Costa? And how many more of them were there? He must discover the answers to these questions, or the streets wouldn't be safe. Starting tomorrow, he'd cast his net far and wide to see if his spies had heard anything.

He popped above the water to be greeted by a scream. His maid Eva's wide eyes latched onto him above the pile of towels she was carrying.

"Master Tomel! You scared me. I didn't realize you were here."

Curse women and their damned reactions! Their infernal squeals would be the death of him.

"Take yourself in hand, girl, and give me a blessed towel!" He winced as Eva jumped and hurried across to the bath, a fresh towel held out and eyes averted. The Goddess knew he wasn't used to the delicacies of women after being raised amongst six brothers. The situation had molded his mother into a woman more than capable of holding her own with her men. James recalled many a time when Mother had waded into the middle of her fighting sons, grabbing two by the ears and elbowing the rest out of her way.

He stood and wrapped the towel around his middle, then grabbed another to dry himself.

"I'm sorry, Sir, I don't know what's gotten into me." Eva continued toward the washstand where she deposited the remaining towels. She turned to leave and let out a strangled cry.

"Ahhhh!" The girl doubled over, clutching at her stomach, and, as a cold wave of fear washed over James, clear fluid gushed down the girl's legs. She screamed and dropped to her knees.

"I'm leaking! Is it the babe?"

For a second, he froze in mind and body, but then he was moving, grabbing towels to place under the girl. "Rest on these while I get help, Eva. No need to panic. If the babe is coming, we'll deal with it."

"It's too early! It can't be coming."

"Eva," he said, his voice firm. "Stay calm. You won't help the child by getting upset. Breathe and I'll be back as soon as I can." He left the room and bolted for the kitchen.

* * *

Kat battled a night hound, but this time the dog and its pack surrounded her, and there was no James to help. Magic should be able to save her if she could summon it.

There was a barrier between her and the glowing golden source that lay within. She tried again to reach it, to block out the hounds, and believe in herself, but a loud knocking distracted her. Was it the frantic beat of her heart? Or the drums summoning her to her eternal reward? Reward? She had the presence of mind to realize she didn't deserve any reward.

Rough hands shook Kat awake. She came out fighting, batting at the groping hands.

"Miss Katrine, it's me, Harah!"

"Harah? What's wrong?" Kat struggled to shake off the dream and the fear.

"There's a man here - Master Tomel the jeweler. He says he needs your help."

"Oh, more night hounds I suppose." Kat climbed from the bed and pulled on her breeches and shirt.

Harah frowned. "What's this talk of night hounds?"

"Oh…" She was a ninny and half asleep still. "Just talking rubbish. I must have been having a nightmare."

"I don't like the idea of you going into the night with a man, even one as respectable as Master Tomel." Harah stood wringing her hands. "What would your sister say?"

What indeed? Kat could imagine Esta being overjoyed - happily shoving her at the first man who called. No, that wasn't true. Esta cared for her and wished only for her happiness, but Kat also knew her melancholy weighed on Esta. She'd be grateful if a man could make Kat happy. *Listen to me! My head is a mess! Silly, silly woman!*

"No need to be concerned, Harah. All will be well. I shall send you word in the morning."

Kat squeezed the older woman's shoulder and slipped from the room. She retrieved her cloak from a hook near the front door and slipped out into the street. James was a shadowy figure, standing by his trap and pony.

"You came!" he said, reaching out and helping her up onto the seat of his cart. "I worried it might be too much to ask." He hauled himself up beside her.

"I don't know what you want, James, but when someone asks for help at this hour, it's usually urgent."

"That it is. My maid Eva is having her babe. You were the only person I could think of."

Kat couldn't help her squeak of dismay. "Birthing a child? I have no experience with that! Well, except for calves and piglets, but it's hardly the same thing. Where's the midwife?"

James failed to look at her, but it was too dark to see his face anyway. "The midwife can't be found, and Mistress Lary needs help."

"Well then, your mother, or a sister? There must be someone other than me!" Even the Crystal Chamber hadn't scared her this much.

"I don't have a sister, only six brothers, and my mother is too far away. You will cope with the ordeal fine if your encounter with the night hound is any indication."

"This is different, James. This is responsibility for the life of another being."

He released his grip on the reins and held her shaking hands, the warmth penetrating her skin like fire. It was nice on this cold night, comforting. His mention of the legendary creature had her peering into the dark alleys they passed, but the sure step of the pony reassured her there was nothing to fear there - not at the moment.

She closed her eyes, huddled in her cloak, and tried to accept James's faith in her wasn't misplaced. He was only fetching her to hold the maid's hand, not to do any real delivering. All would be well. Soon there'd be a new life, and she could return to the cottage. It was about time she got Claus and Harah packed up and on their way before James dragged her into any more danger. Already, she was enjoying holding his hand a little too much. As if he discerned her thoughts, he squeezed her hands, but, when she glanced across at him, she found him concentrating on the road ahead.

The little cart bounced along at such a brisk pace it was no time before they arrived at James's manor house. He helped her down from the conveyance, and ushered her up the steps and into the entry of the house. A shrill scream sounded from within. Kat froze and pulled her hand from his grasp.

"I don't want to do this. Please, there must be another alternative." Her body trembled like she had a fever, and she tasted bile.

"Women have an instinct when it comes to birthing babies. Come, even if you only hold her hand."

Kat hung back, her arms across her middle. "Not *this* woman. I have no instinct; not for this." Hetty had never taught her aught about delivering a babe and nor had her mother.

But James again grasped her hand and drew her down a hall to a room at the end. He knocked and opened the door, pulling Kat with him and closing the door behind them. She froze again as she took in the sight before her. A young woman lay on the big bed - James's she assumed - her belly round with child, her legs apart, and her modesty protected only by a thin towel. As she watched, an older woman raised the towel, and Kat saw more than she wanted to see of the birthing channel. Was it the babe's head that protruded from between the mounds of flesh?

The girl screamed again, snapping Kat out of her horror and propelling her toward the bed. "Get out if you are going to stand gawking," she said to James as she dropped her coat and cloak across a chair and rolled up her sleeves. "What can I do, Mistress?" she asked of the older woman, Mistress Lary she presumed.

She looked back at Kat with wide eyes. It seemed she was out of her depth as James had declared. "Have you seen a babe born, girl?"

Kat shook her head.

"Then hold her hand and talk to her, encourage her, do anything you can think of to soothe her fear."

Kat did as she was told, sitting behind the pregnant girl and encouraging her to relax against her chest. "My name is Katrine, Eva."

"It's too soon," Eva said. "Too soon."

Kat wanted to ask so many questions but none would help the girl. Instead, she cursed the day she came across James Tomel. "Your babe is strong, and he has decided now is the time. You must trust in him."

Eva looked at her with desperate eyes that knew an echo within Kat. "How can you be sure?"

She bit down on a whimper. "I know it."

Mistress Lary placed her hand on Eva's belly. "When the next contraction comes you must push hard. That will deliver the head, and soon you'll hold your child."

Eva sobbed. "I'm so tired. I don't think I can push anymore."

"Yes you can," Kat said, "you can push for as long as you need to. I have faith in you."

At Kat's words, the girl appeared to calm, and her breathing deepened. Then another contraction hit.

"You can do this," Kat said. "Push as hard as you can, now!"

Kat had to give Eva credit, for she did push as hard as she had energy for. "One more big push, Eva. Now!"

"The head is delivered," Mistress Lary said. "Good girl."

"You did it," Kat said. "You're almost there."

Kat sought Mistress Lary's eyes and saw only fear there. What was wrong? Dread turned her insides to ice, but she had to be strong, for Eva. "Next contraction you have to give your last big push. Isn't that right, Mistress? Eva will have her babe to hold."

"Yes, girl, not long now."

Tears ran down Mistress Lary's face, but Kat didn't understand what caused them. How could the mistress know anything yet? The babe was not fully born. She gripped Eva's hand.

"Now listen. When your contraction comes you must push."

"I can help now, girl," Mistress Lary said. "Do as Katrine says."

At the next contraction, Eva pushed until she was red in the face, and the next thing Kat knew she was being handed a blue little body - a little girl.

"Rub her then hang her upside down and slap her on the backside, then repeat the process."

Kat did as she was told, but there was no response from the baby. Amid wails from Eva, she laid the child across her lap and breathed gentle puffs of air into her chest as she had seen her farm manager do with piglets. *But I have no skill, no skill!*

The tiny chest scarcely moved. Hands shaking so much she was afraid of dropping the child, Kat patted the tiny back then rolled the infant over for more puffs into its rosebud mouth.

Terror bubbled its way up from the dark place within, stealing her breath, tightening the muscles of her chest and chasing the blood from her extremities. She couldn't let any of that show on her face - for Eva's sake. She had to be strong though all her insides were crumbling. She stopped to draw breath. The soft skin of the child was blue, and there had been no sound.

She shoved the baby at Mistress Lary. "You try!" Kat turned to Eva and drew the girl against her, rocking her and patting her back. She was ashamed to be drawing comfort from the young mother even as she tried to offer support. She delved deep inside to find a spell that might bring life to the baby but, in her panic, she failed to summon any words, any power that might help.

Mistress Lary placed the child across her knees and gave firm pats to her back then rolled her over and pushed on her chest. There was no movement no matter what she did. Finally, she wrapped the baby girl and offered her to Eva.

"I'm sorry, Eva," Mistress Lary said. "There's nothing more I can do. Nurse your daughter while I deliver the afterbirth."

Eva's eyes were so huge, Kat thought she might pass out from shock, so she took the child herself and placed it in the girl's arms. She drew Eva back on the pillows and covered her with a shawl then went to the fire and removed a heated stone.

While the housekeeper went to work, Kat wrapped the hot stone in a towel and placed it under Eva's legs. The girl hadn't said a thing since the babe had been placed in her arms. She lay staring down at the baby as though she didn't understand why it was there.

Kat felt more completely helpless than ever before. She was desperate to flee this room of blood and death and never face it again. Logic told her it was not her fault, but, amidst all this, the cold voice of reason had no place.

Perhaps if she had known more about birth, she might have been able to revive the tiny child. She sighed and drew a chair close to the bed, holding Eva's hand as she waited for reality to strike the young mother.

CHAPTER 5

JAMES paced back and forth in the kitchen, waiting for news from the birthing room. They'd been in there for more than an hour with no indication of how the delivery progressed. It was too early for the child to make an appearance and Eva was young and tiny. Without experienced help, James feared the worst. And he had dragged Katrine into this mess.

As the sun sent the first few rays through the kitchen window, he decided he couldn't wait any longer. He wrenched open the kitchen door only to find Katrine standing outside. The magnificent silver that habitually lit her eyes was dulled by exhaustion and something more. Her shoulders were slumped, and blood stained her tunic.

He drew her into the kitchen and pushed her into a chair, kneeling before her.

"What happened? The babe?"

"Is dead." Her voice was dull, and she sat with her head in her hands.

James placed his hand on her shoulder. She flinched away.

"Why did you bring me here?" Her accusing gaze was upon him. "There was nothing I could do."

"I had no one else to turn to," he protested, forcing himself to meet her eye.

"You could've been there for her yourself," she snapped. "After all, she's your maid, and you've taken responsibility for her."

"How would it appear if I was present? The birthing room is no place for a man!"

"Coward!"

James surged to his feet. "Now see here! I've never shirked my duty." A small voice asked him about the duty he had to his parents, but he shook it off. "I've done all I can for Eva."

She threaded shaking fingers through her hair. "You have no idea what it cost me to be there. I had to try and breathe life into the babe when I have no skill."

He stared, understanding the basis of Katrine's anger. "I'm sorry you had to do that."

"I failed, and I'll never know if it was my fault. Perhaps there was never any hope for the babe, but I can't be sure."

"Katrine," he held her hands tight, though she tried to wrench them from his grasp. "I'm truly sorry. I'll do whatever it takes to help you. Of course, it goes without saying that I'll continue to care for Eva. She'll always be welcome here."

"I want you to take me home."

"Of course. I'll get you something to eat while I check on Eva and prepare the trap." James crossed to the fire where a kettle was boiling and made a pot of tea. He delivered a steaming mug to Katrine along with a thick slab of fresh buttered bread and honey. He left the kitchen, her accusation every bit as forceful as the stinging slap she had delivered to him only two days ago.

* * *

Kat sat on a cushion in front of the fireplace in her room. She had been there all day since returning from James's mansion. He must've explained what happened, for Harah had delivered two meals during the day, patted her shoulder, and left without a word. There *were* no words to fix what was broken inside.

She told herself all day that time would lessen her grief at the death of Eva's daughter, but only a small part of her believed it. How could she ever forget the feel of the small body in her arms - or the weight

42

of the responsibility? Failure was too insignificant a word for what had transpired in that room. How could she ever get past this?

There was nothing she'd been taught that would help. *I wish Hetty was here.* The old witch knew so much about life. She had been her savior after the events in the Crystal Cave when Kat almost had the life burned out of her.

Her magical powers were greatly enhanced by the experience, but so was her melancholy. And magic wouldn't help her in this situation. It hadn't helped with the birth of the child. *I should have been able to summon a spell that would start that tiny heart!*

Hetty…she might be able to help, and it was some time since Kat had contacted her. A desperate longing to speak to her friend and mentor now drove her to the wood stack in the corner. She built up the fire until it was roaring and sat before it, eyes closed. In her mind, she built an image of Hetty, feature by feature. She smiled at the familiar scowl the old woman often presented to the world - and to her.

"What's the meaning of this interruption, child?"

Kat's eyes flew open. Hetty's image danced before her in the flames. She was none too happy, and Kat noticed changes that caused a spike of fear in her gut.

"I wanted to see you again, speak to you," she said, ashamed of her wavering voice.

"You might have chosen a better time! I'm in my bed!"

Disturbing indeed when Hetty normally kept hours like an owl. The witch shoved a skeletal hand through her wild, wispy hair. *She has lost so much weight!*

"I…" How to ask the myriad of questions that rushed to mind?

"Spit it out, Kat! You look as though a ghost has walked over your grave."

She flinched at the mention of ghosts and graves, and Hetty's sharp eyes noticed.

"Is there something wrong with your sister? Your mother?"

She shook her head. "Nothing like that. I've had…a difficult night…and I wanted to talk it over with you. But I see you aren't well. What's wrong?"

Hetty opened her mouth to speak, but a hacking cough robbed her of her words. When she finished, she lay back on her pillow, her chest rising and falling at an alarming rate. "Give me a moment to catch my breath, child."

Kat's body began to shake. Hetty was ill and with no one to take care of her. What if she should die? The old witch was tough, but Kat had never seen her sick before, let alone bed ridden.

"I have a little cold, that's all. Don't fret, I'll soon be right as rain. I just need my rest."

"And I'm disturbing it. I'm sorry, Hetty, I would never wish to do you harm."

"Don't listen to the crotchety comments of an old woman, child. Tell me, what's the matter?"

Kat drew a deep breath and explained everything that had happened over the last few days, ending with the death of the babe. She also explained her deepest fears.

"You know I have this terrible melancholy inside me since the Crystal Cave, Hetty. Nothing I do will shift it. I have no joy in life, I merely try to keep moving from one chore to another. If I keep busy, it's better. Now I fear even being busy will be no help."

"My poor girl," Hetty said, her dark eyes softer than Kat had ever seen them. "The babe – that's the circle of life. We are born, and we die. The child's lungs weren't ready to breathe. There was nothing the most skilled midwife could've done to save her - nothing the strongest spell could have changed. You must accept the will of the Goddess. But I'm not saying it will be easy." Hetty settled back on the pillow again, eyes closed.

"Hetty?" Kat's voice rose and she struggled to bring it back under control. "Are you well?"

"A moment, child," she wheezed. "…need to catch my breath again."

It was worse than Kat had thought. Hetty was never short of breath.

"The night hound," Hetty said at last, her hand rubbing her breastbone. "That's serious. It may have been drawn to your magic. I haven't heard of them for at least fifty years. You need to take care. Try not to use sorcery, and, if you do, invert the spell to lower the chance of detection. You remember how to do that, don't you?"

Kat nodded. "Of course, but I never practice it."

"Well, get it straight in your mind how you do it. But, whatever you do, don't practice it now. If I'm right, it could draw every night hound for thirty miles." Each short sentence sucked more life from her. She drew a deep breath that had her hacking up again.

"Your melancholy will pass," Hetty said. "Don't surrender to it." She coughed again then wiped her mouth with a handkerchief. "You need people around you. Who is your closest friend?"

Kat had to think about the question. "Esta, my sister."

"Who else?"

"My mother?"

"Do you have a man?" Hetty's voice was hoarse. Kat could hardly hear her now.

"Of course not!" *I don't need a man.*

"A pity, child. A man can come in dashed handy at times."

Kat didn't believe what she was hearing. "*You* don't have a fellow, Hetty. How have you managed?"

"You know me not at all. I've had more than my share of men and outlived them all. There have been hard times, and, but for the support of friends, I wouldn't be here speaking to you now."

Kat couldn't think how to respond to those statements which seemed irrelevant to her right in that moment. She experienced an aching sadness for Hetty though, all alone in her sickness. "I will think on what you've said - and I'm coming to look after you."

Hetty's eyes widened in alarm, and a massive coughing fit seized her. Kat looked on, helpless to do anything and mortified she had caused this distress.

When the old woman's cough subsided, she sat up in bed, her hand outstretched. "You must promise me not to come, child. It's too dangerous."

"Hetty—"

"Promise! I can't lie here worrying about you on the road with elves, and night hounds, and the Goddess only knows what dangers. I remember how impulsive you are. Don't come to Brightcastle!"

Kat was again lost for words. She couldn't sit here in comfort when her friend might be dying. But Hetty wouldn't rest if she thought Kat was risking herself. She would have to lie and make it damned convincing.

"If you're certain you're on the mend, I promise. But only if you're certain."

"I *am* on the mend, child. I've looked after myself since before you were born. Stay where you are, and I can rest quietly knowing you're safe."

Kat didn't like to lie, however, in this case, she had no choice. "Very well. Please get well soon. I promise to hold all your advice close to my heart." *And I'll be at your bedside as soon as is humanly possible.*

Hetty's image faded from the flames, and a shiver ran up Kat's spine. The room was suddenly frigid without the old woman's company.

Kat got up from the fireplace, fetched her saddlebags, and began stuffing her clothes into them.

CHAPTER 6

JAMES pulled his pony and trap up to the front of the feed store and climbed down. One of his mares had taken ill, and the shop owner here had potions he hoped might be helpful.

He scowled as he tied the pony to the rail. He'd never get his projects finished at this rate - what with night hounds, and Eva's disastrous birth, and now a sick horse - he hadn't finished any significant pieces of jewelry for weeks.

He stepped up onto the front porch of the store and was about to pass through the swinging doors when a flurry of dark hair and tunic clad arms ran into him. He almost went down in a heap but caught himself, and the lady in question - one hand on the door frame and one around her waist.

"What the demon are you doing?" he asked. "Charging around like the hounds of hell are on your tail. I could've injured you!"

"Good day to you too, Master Tomel," Katrine said, the silver flecks in her eyes sparkling in the sunlight, before a cloud chased the life from her eyes. "How is Eva?"

"As well as can be expected under the circumstances." James would never forget the sight of poor Eva cradling her dead baby. "In the end, we had to forcibly remove the child. I admit to being unsure how to help, however, the midwife came, and she and Mistress Lary have been wonderful."

"That's good to hear."

He couldn't help noticing the movement of her throat as she swallowed. "Are you well?" he asked.

She drew herself up, shoulders back, and looked him in the eye. The sparkles in her eyes swirled hypnotically. "I'm fine. I was upset yesterday, but today I feel better."

James realized she wasn't as fine as she asserted. Goddess, he wasn't, and he hadn't gone through the harrowing ordeal that Katrine had. However, he had no choice but to take her at her word.

"Then I shall be on my way. May the Goddess keep you safe." He bowed and stepped around her.

"I wish I could say it's been a pleasure, but we both know it wouldn't be true."

He turned at her words and watched as she strode to her horse. It was only then he noticed the animal was loaded for travel with bulging saddle bags. She was tying what looked like a bag of oats across his rump.

"Wait a moment," he said. "Where are you going?"

If he was right, the lady was supposed to be helping the old Delacost couple prepare to move north.

She turned to face him. "I'm departing this morning for Brightcastle, not that it's any concern of yours. I have a friend who is ill and needs my care."

"You said nothing of this yesterday."

"As if I had the chance to. Besides, what I do is none of your concern." She stood with hands on hips, statuesque in her form-fitting breeches and tunic. She'd draw the attention of every rogue on the journey.

He approached her, determined at first to talk her out of the trip. But why should he interfere? This was Katrine's decision, and she could handle herself somewhat. Still, he couldn't leave the matter alone. "Who are you traveling with?"

She looked down her nose at him, though he was taller than her by a head. "No one." She turned and mounted her spirited stallion who stamped and tossed his head. "Demon will take care of me. He's a trained war horse."

Impossible! Walk away, man. She doesn't want your help. "I can't allow you to travel to Brightcastle by yourself. At least take an escort. Mason! He can accompany you."

"Mason is needed to move my friends. Now get out of my way."

She turned her horse and proceeded up the street at a brisk walk. *She's going to get herself killed!* It was at least a five-day ride, and the weather hadn't started to warm yet. Add to that the risk of bandits, night hounds and dark elves, and it was sheer lunacy for Katrine to travel by herself. *But it's not your concern!*

He jogged after her, nonetheless. "Lady Aranati! Lady Katrine!" People were looking at him, noting how the master jeweler ran up the street after a woman. "Wait!"

She stopped again and waited for him to come alongside. "What is it now?"

"If you delay your start, I'll see you have an escort."

She frowned at him. "You can't interfere in my life like this."

Does she have no concept of danger? "Look, Lady, it's not safe for you to travel alone, especially not with those creatures on the prowl." He was rewarded by a look of unease on her lovely face. "Wait while I organize some guards. I have a few at my disposal."

Her mouth hung open. She appeared lost for words.

"Is that agreement?" he snapped.

She sighed. "Very well. Organize your guards, and I'll wait for them at that tavern." She pointed to one of the better establishments in the town and rode away.

* * *

Kat sipped an ale as she waited for James's guards. She had already been here two hours. Long enough to polish off a fish pie and warm herself by the fire. She had also endured more than one proposition from other patrons. In the end, her hunting knife, placed on the table before her, kept them away.

She sighed, swallowed the last of the ale, replaced the knife in her boot, and stood. Time to be on the road, or she'd have to spend another night on the trail. Kat pushed open the door and strode to Demon. She removed his nosebag and stowed it under the bag of oats, then mounted him. An icy wind made her draw her wool lined cloak around her. It would be a cold trip over the next week.

As she heeled her horse away from the inn, she spied a horse-drawn dray and six armed men coming down the street. On the seat of the dray was James.

"I see I was right to worry you wouldn't wait." His broad shoulders were hidden under a heavy cloak, but nothing could mask the magnetism of the man. Kat didn't understand how he was only a tradesman. He looked so much more dangerous. And why had the Goddess sent him to pester her?

"I've waited over two hours, jeweler. What are *you* doing here? You said guards."

"I got to thinking. It's not right for a lady to go off with armed guards, so I'm offering myself as part of the escort. I promised I'd see Princess Benae of Brightcastle to fit her for a coronet. And I have someone else I need to visit as well."

She wouldn't ask him who. She didn't care. It looked like the thorn in her side wasn't so easily dislodged. "What about your responsibilities here? Your business, your staff, Eva?"

He shrugged. "My staff will take care of themselves and everything else."

Was he running away? Was *she*? Lately she had seized the chance to escape her life at each opportunity. That goal had brought her to Costa and, in part, drove her to Brightcastle.

She gave him one last glare and set herself on the path out of Costa, riding west.

* * *

James admired the woman on the horse in front of him. She seemed determined to keep her distance, riding a good ten paces in front. Well, let her! He didn't need to be by her side to protect her. He kept asking himself why he had changed his plans and come on this trek. He was never impulsive, and there was a mountain of work awaiting him at home. He shook his head and thumped his thigh with a fist.

One of the guards, Dael, rode close to the dray. "Who is the chit, Master Tomel?"

James flicked a look his way. "Someone I met on the road and keep running into."

The man grinned. "I can see why you keep running into her."

James ground his teeth. Dael was always free with his opinions. "Keep your eyes on the forest, man." This seemed a worse idea by the minute. And it would be damned uncomfortable sleeping rough tonight. At least tomorrow there would be an inn where they could spend the night.

* * *

Kat reined in her horse and turned off the road toward a clearing she had used before on her journeys to Brightcastle. She didn't much care what James did. This was her trip he had muscled his way into, and she would damned well decide where they camped.

It took only ten minutes to arrive at her destination, and she paused to survey the clearing with its fire pit and thick bed of pine needles.

She dismounted and tied Demon to a tree on the edge of the clearing, then placed his nosebag on. She removed his saddle then rubbed him down, so his coat shone. By the time she brought her saddle and gear back to the clearing, James and his six guards had set up the camp.

She stood with hands on hips and surveyed the camp before meeting James's gaze.

"I trust this meets with your approval?" she said. *Damn it! Why did I have to say that?* As if she cared about his approval!

One side of his mouth quirked up. "Isn't it early to stop for the night?"

"It's early, but the next suitable clearing is three more hours ride, and, by then, it will be dark."

"I happen to know of several I would've told you about had you cared to ask." James had unhitched the horse from the dray and was rubbing him down.

"Oh," Kat said. "Well, I've already bedded my horse down so this will have to do."

Four guards saw to the horses while the other two soon had a meal cooking over the fire. Kat lay back on her bed roll and watched the efficiency with which they went about their chores. The six were a well-oiled team.

She stood and retrieved a towel from her saddle bags. "I'm going to wash up before dinner." She pointed into the forest. "There's a stream a short walk through there."

Kat fetched a water bag and left without further explanation. She was soon at the creek and filled the water bag before stripping off her shirt and breeches. She removed her boots and socks and stood in the cold water using a smaller towel to wash off the dust of the road. The sun sent its last rays into the forest, silent except for the running water. Her skin pebbled with goosebumps as she completed her wash and dried herself with the larger towel. It felt good to be clean. She was sitting on a rock drying her feet when a whisper of sound alerted her to an intruder.

Kat stood and turned, expecting one of the men. Fear surged through her at the sight of the night hound perched on a rock above. It was at least as large as the one she had fought in Costa, but its short coat was black. Red eyes gleamed at her and saliva dripped from savage canine teeth. Rather than give herself over to fear, she reached within to the roiling pool of anger which was never far away.

"Hound of hell," she said. "Back up and leave this place for I can fry you where you stand." She gathered her power, sensed it well up from within, and prepared to launch a fireball. Kat met the baleful scarlet eyes of the hound and held its stare as the fire built within. Just a few more seconds… She drew her right arm back, then whipped it forward as the beast leaped. A fireball the size of a small boulder hit the beast, and Kat dived to the side to avoid the burning creature as it flew past and into the stream. She rolled over in time to see the hound floating away, thrashing in agony, steam rolling off it as the water quenched the flames. A tormented howl echoed across the rocky stream as the hound disappeared.

She gritted her teeth to stifle the cry that rose from her gut. Again, savage grief struck, and she covered her face with her hands, sucking in deep breaths, fighting her reaction to killing the hound. Something within her rebelled against killing these creatures, but why? She had killed men before and never experienced this desperate sadness.

"Katrine! Are you well?" James stood above her, his gaze unfathomable in the darkening forest. "I heard a howl."

She pushed herself to her feet, still breathing deeply to bring her turbulent feelings under control. *He must not know I can defend myself with magic. He'll never understand.*

"Another of the hounds," she said, pulling on her shirt and keeping her face averted. "I managed to dodge it, and it was carried away in the stream."

He jumped down and stood before her, his eyes scorching up her bare legs. Kat shivered. They were rivals, but she wondered how it could be between them. There was something primal in him that called to her. She thought he must feel it too by the look he gave her. *Better get your breeches on woman!*

She dressed and pulled on her boots, all the while conscious of his eyes on her.

"Tell me what happened." His voice was low, determined, and suspicious.

She turned on him. "It's gone!" She stormed past him and back toward the camp. "We must prepare for more."

* * *

James sat wrapped in his own thoughts. Katrine was asleep in the dray. That had been a monumental battle. He wouldn't allow her to sleep on the ground when there was an elevated platform to hand. Of course, he had planned to join her, but she curtailed those plans with one well directed look. He had meant nothing by the suggestion - merely sharing a space. She glared at him as if he was the worst libertine in recorded history.

Not that intimacy with her hadn't crossed his mind. She was beautiful and the glimpse of her long legs before she had pulled on her breeches made him hard. *Totally inappropriate!* To distract himself from the thought of her legs, James pondered what had occurred with the hound. She didn't wish to tell him how the beast had landed in the water; and there was the distinct odor of burning hair and flesh. He shook his head. Where had the smell come from? He had searched the banks of the stream and found nothing to explain it. And he hadn't imagined her distress when he had found her on the bank of the stream. What was she hiding?

James didn't like things he didn't understand, and he most definitely had no understanding of Katrine or the blasted hounds. Why was a beast not seen in the kingdom in half a century now stalking them? One thing was certain. If the hounds kept trailing them, sooner or later someone might die. Two of his guards slept beside him - he didn't understand how they were able to wrap themselves in their cloaks and sleep as if they hadn't a care in the world - and the other four patrolled the forest surrounding them, though two of them stationed themselves in trees on his suggestion.

James suspected he wouldn't get a wink of sleep this night, between thinking of a certain bewitching woman and worrying about his guards out there, placing themselves at risk. He paid them well and they knew the risks of their profession. He had warned them of the added danger of the night hounds. However, he would blame himself if any one of them was harmed.

As he lay, ears straining for foreign night sounds, James pondered the changes in his world over the last few days. Katrine Aranati was the catalyst of all the events - well most of them. He couldn't blame her for Eva's pregnancy and disastrous birth. But the rest... he had no experience of women like her and suspected there *was* no one like her. She rode like a man, dressed like a man, had the face of a goddess from his most erotic fantasies, and there was a world of pain in her extraordinary eyes. He wanted to discover more, but that would be inviting chaos into his previously ordered existence. Besides, he wasn't free to pursue anything. No, he would see her safely to Brightcastle then banish her from his mind forever. In fact, he needed to stop thinking of her right now.

James rolled over and closed his eyes for the hundredth time, but nothing could shut out the picture of the hauntingly beautiful Katrine Aranati.

CHAPTER 7

K AT sat up in the dray and stretched her arms above her head. The chill air sent a shiver down her spine. It was quiet, the dawn light beginning to filter through the trees, and there should've been bird sounds. She shuffled to the edge of the wagon, pulling her cloak about her as she went. Her boots hit the dirt of the clearing with a soft thud.

Searching for James, she saw his bed empty, the blankets scattered. A guard stood silent at the far side of the clearing - he raised a finger to his lips.

She struggled to swallow the lump in her throat. What was afoot? She pulled her powers to the fore, seizing them in case she needed to defend herself, and approached the guard.

"What's amiss?" she hissed.

"Hendel didn't return from guard duty, Lady." The man's eyes flickered to her and back to his surroundings. "The others are looking for him."

She drew a deep breath. "Do you think it's the hounds?"

"Heard nothing, Lady."

Damn him! Surely he had more to report. She surveyed the clearing. Nothing seemed amiss. One of the horses nickered, and Kat crossed to their lines and spoke quietly to them, rubbing each nose as she passed. They all settled except Demon who fixed her with a fierce eye and tossed his head. Let a night hound tangle with him and it would know what for! He had no fear of anything, unlike her.

She scanned the surrounding forest as she fetched her saddle and returned to Demon. No matter how this was resolved, they'd depart quickly. She placed two handfuls of oats in his nosebag and attached it, then did the same for the other horses. The guard joined her and began saddling the animals, his eyes on his surroundings.

"You work here," she said. "I'll keep a look out."

His smirk faded as she grasped the bole of the nearest tree and shimmied up until she was the height of a ship's mast above the forest floor. *Damn him!* She settled on a branch and methodically checked each quadrant of the forest. In the last, she spied movement. *James!* And the other guards; carrying a bundle. *Wait!* There were only four guards with him. Fear struck her gut. It was a body they carried - a man's body.

She hastened from her lofty perch and landed beside the horses. "They come!" she said to the guard. "I think they found Hendel. This way!" She pulled his sleeve and set off across the clearing into the trees on the other side. They had only gone a dozen yards when they spied the somber procession.

Kat froze while the guard pushed past. "Ho, Master Tomel!"

James's head snapped up. "Dael! Where's Katrine?"

"I'm here," she said.

The wariness on his face turned to relief. He must care a little. "Get back to the clearing! Prepare your mounts for travel."

And then she saw Hendel - or what was left of him. One side of his face was gone, and there was a gaping hole in his chest as though his heart had been ripped out. She staggered back as the guards carrying him approached and would have fallen if not for James's outstretched hand. She spun and emptied her stomach onto the pine needles while James held her hair back, his arm around her waist.

"What happened?' she asked, though she knew the answer.

"By the prints around the body, I'd say it was the hounds, perhaps two or three. He never stood a chance. Wasn't much of a struggle, so I don't think he saw them until it was too late."

Kat looked up at him, noting the greyness of his skin. "Why? Why do they hunt us?"

"Your guess is as good as mine." His eyes searched her, drilled right into her soul. "Perhaps your guess may be better than mine. I never saw them until they were chasing *you*."

"You can't seriously think I have anything to do with those hounds!"

He gripped her upper arms. "Tell me why they're hunting you!"

"They aren't hunting me," she said through gritted teeth. *I can't reveal anything of my magic to him.* Magic powers were a gift you hid, not held up as a banner for all to see. Besides, she wasn't sure if her magic had anything to do with the hounds. Even Hetty wasn't completely certain. Despite that, she'd take care not to use sorcery again if she could possibly avoid it. And she'd invert any spells she did need to use. It certainly appeared the hounds were dogging her steps and she'd take no more risks - well, only calculated risks.

James frowned, his eyes searching her face as if desperate to trust her. *Huh! Master James Tomel is many things but desperate isn't one of them.*

"There's a man dead!" he snapped. "You need to tell me if you have more information about these beasts."

She shook her head. "I've told you all I know. You have to believe me."

He let go of one of her arms and led her back to the clearing where Hendel's body lay. She averted her eyes from the gore.

"We need to get out of here," James said. "Two of you take the body back to Costa. The rest of us will push on to Brightcastle."

There was a howl of protest from the five guards, demanding the expedition be aborted. Kat drew herself up and folded her arms across her chest. *I'm not afraid, and nothing will stop me from getting to Hetty!*

James turned to her. "Perhaps we should return to Costa while only one of us lies dead. As it is, I have no idea how I'll explain this to Hendel's family."

Sorrow struck at Kat like a physical blow. She knew what it was like to lose a loved one - she missed her father every day - but that was a reason for continuing. She could never live with herself if Hetty passed away and she did nothing. "I understand how you must feel, and my heart is heavy for Hendel and his folk. I don't expect any of you to help me." She deliberately addressed the last sentence to James. "However, I intend to continue on to Brightcastle. There's an inn I can sleep in tonight and perhaps on my own I can pass undetected by the hounds."

She believed she could thwart any attack that came against her, but if her magic really drew them…She shuddered at the vision of the creatures chasing her all the way to her destination.

James shook his head. "I can't let you go on alone. What kind of a man do you think I am?"

Kat stared at him, wondering if he would really try to stop her from seeing Hetty. *Over my dead body!* She turned to the guards who eyed her with varying degrees of hostility.

"Look," she said to them all. "Each of you must make a choice. But know this: I don't expect any of you to come with me. It was never my plan. You all have people depending on you." She drew a deep breath. "And so do I. There is a sick old woman in Brightcastle with no one to care for her. She needs me, and I won't let her down."

* * *

James sat on the seat of the dray, his thoughts drifting like a leaf in a stream. He blamed lack of sleep on his hare-brained decision to continue with Katrine. She rode alongside, on Demon, also lost in her thoughts. Two guards accompanied them - the rest had returned with Hendel. He had to believe they'd be safe.

He was sure Katrine had something to do with the hounds though she denied it. She seemed sincere in her rejection of the idea, but, as far as James was concerned, it was fact. Just as important was another question only *he* could answer. Why had he decided to continue on? The other men were swayed by his decision, and their devotion cut him.

And Katrine! She was the most stubborn woman he'd ever met, but along with his frustration came a grudging respect. She was scared, but she wasn't allowing her fear to defeat her. It certainly appeared she was made of better stuff than her sister! His eyes strayed to her shapely legs as they guided Demon. Everything about the woman intrigued him - her beauty, her toughness, her heart, and her capability. And there was something else - a compelling, bewitching quality.

His heart shuddered. *Bewitching!* Was *that* it? Was Katrine a practitioner of the magical arts? It would explain much - her eyes, the night hounds, and her strange vanquishing of the beast at the stream. Magical ability would lend her courage, for she'd clearly be able to defend herself better than most women. She held herself apart from others, almost as if she walked upon a different world. Yes, if Katrine was a witch it would make sense of much that had transpired over the last four days.

The thought should scare him, even repulse him, but James was surprised to discover it did not. If this woman was a practitioner of magic, it only added to her mystery, her attraction. He shook his head. Instead of escorting her to Brightcastle, he should be turning her into the king and running far in the other direction. The truth was he had never been drawn to anyone as he was to Katrine. A large part of him urged him to take a chance and see where his acquaintance with her might lead. He ignored it, of course. His future lay elsewhere than with this captivating but chaotic young woman.

* * *

It was late in the day, and Kat's head pounded with questions she had no answers for. How would they make it unscathed to Brightcastle and Hetty? Why did James continue to keep her company, let alone his two men? When would the next hound attack them? How could they survive another three nights on the road?

She shook her head and tried to focus on anything other than her predicament. She and James rode side by side on the seat of his dray. Demon had sensed her inner turmoil and started prancing, leading James to offer up a seat on his wagon. It had been a mistake to accept.

His muscular thigh rubbed up against hers, and, each time it did, something low in her belly squirmed and her nipples tingled. She had never felt anything like this before, despite having exchanged kisses with more than one willing man in the past.

She had never taken a man to her bed but was well acquainted with what happened. Might James be her first? Her body heated at the thought of him naked. Her mouth went dry imagining what he might look like under his clothes. And then his thigh bumped her again, and she almost jumped off the seat.

"Are you well?" His deep voice vibrated through her, all the way to her toes.

She turned to him, bringing his mouth dangerously close to hers, and forced her eyes up to his. That didn't help as his dark stare reminded her of the black places in dangerously hot flames.

Kat sighed and swallowed the urge to press her lips against his. "I'm tired, that's all."

"Are you sure? You've been so quiet."

"So have you."

He looked ahead. "I've been trying to understand what I'm doing here."

"You didn't need to come with me, James."

"I realize that, but I couldn't let you ride off on your own."

She frowned. "I can take care of myself. I don't need you. I don't need anyone."

"Perhaps that's what intrigues me about you." His eyes were upon her again. "You're like a small island in a raging sea. Separate and self-contained."

"You make me sound horrible!"

He placed his hand on her knee, and she jumped. He squeezed, and her cheeks heated - not to mention what her heart did. Damn him! She must stop reacting like this!

"You aren't horrible, but I suspect you're hiding more than one secret." The silence between them stretched. "Am I right?"

"Wha…what do you mean?" He couldn't know what she was. And, if he did, what then?

"Your eyes…the night hounds…the second attack and the burned smell." He took a deep breath and his eyes bored into her. "Are you a witch?"

A chill ran through Kat as she scrambled to decide what to tell him. He was little more than a stranger. Did she trust him enough to reveal this secret part of herself? He had thrown his lot in with her, at least for a short while. Did that mean she owed him at least part of the truth? *You don't owe him this!*

The moment stretched until she realized she had missed her opportunity to deny his accusation. What would change if he knew the truth? What might he do with *that* information?

Kat straightened her shoulders, refusing to meet his gaze, afraid of what she might find there - fear, disgust, revulsion? "I am."

She sensed him stiffen, heard his indrawn breath.

"What does that mean?" he asked.

She sighed. "I have certain powers. Much of my magic relates to potions and spells but I can summon balls of fire, powerful ones. It was how I defeated the second night hound. I wish you'd keep this to yourself, James."

He turned to her. "You think I'd tell anyone this? *I* can barely accept what you are, let alone tell anyone and expect them to treat me the same afterward." They traveled in uncomfortable silence for a time.

Kat wondered if she might awake one morning to find him gone and was surprised to feel dread at the thought. She had always traveled alone before and thought nothing of it.

"Why are those creatures following you?" he asked.

She went cold at the question. "I don't yet know if they are."

"How can you say that? I never saw them until you arrived in Costa, and, now, where you are, they are."

She went to speak then snapped her mouth shut. Were they hunting her? And if so, why? Hetty had said magic might attract the hounds but that didn't explain everything.

"I used magic before the first hound chased me."

"I knew it!"

"Stop jumping to conclusions! I've never seen one before. Why now is it my fault?"

"We have to assume your magic is the source of our trouble. I forbid you to use it again until we reach the city."

How dare he? This was exactly why she avoided relationships. "My magic might be the only thing standing between us and death, Master High and Mighty. What will you say then?"

James looked away to the west where the sun was setting behind the trees. "Truthfully? I don't know what to say. You're right. We can't discount the possibility we might need sorcery against those beasts. However, I don't approve." He fell into a brooding silence, focused on the road ahead.

"I'm a normal woman, you know," she said, her voice barely a whisper on the wind.

James laughed. "Oh, lady. You're so much more than a normal woman." His voice dwindled into contemplation.

Kat wished he'd just say what was eating at him. She was sick of wondering what he wasn't saying. But did it matter? Once they reached Brightcastle, they'd go their separate ways, never to meet again. The thought made her sadder than ever.

Two hours later, with the full moon lighting their way, they arrived at a small roadside inn. The guards stabled the horses and secured the dray while Kat and James entered the establishment's bar. It was crowded with woodsmen and smelled of sweat and ale.

Kat took a seat at the only vacant table while James spoke with the innkeeper. The speculative stares of several rough-looking men made Kat wish she had remained outside.

James joined her with four ales. "There's only one proper room left," he said. "You must take it, and I'll share the loft with the guards."

She clutched his hand. "Stay with me, James. I don't like the looks those men are sending my way."

James surveyed the room and turned back to her. "I see what you mean, but what of your reputation if I share your room?"

"Do you think I care about that when I'm being drooled over by them?" She licked lips which had gone dry and his eyes followed the movement. "Stay with me tonight."

"When you put it like that, how can I refuse?"

Kat drew her hand away from his as their companions joined them, and she passed an uncomfortable half hour eating dinner under the speculative stares of the inn patrons. The tension within built until she could stand it no longer. She pushed her chair back and stood. The room hushed as her chair scraped across the floorboards.

"I'm going up," she said. "Please bring my things."

James stood too. "It's the second room on the right from the top of the stairs. I need to check the horses. I won't be long."

She pushed through the men between her and the stairs, expecting their fingers to grope her at any moment, and glad when she avoided molestation. However relieved she was, the sex-starved stares of the men bore into her as she ascended the steps to the upper rooms. She found her door and pushed it open, stepped through and slammed it behind her. She rested against the inside of the door and waited for her heart to stop its thumping, her hands to quit their shaking.

There was warmish water in the jug, so she shed her outer clothes and washed the dirt of the road from her skin. A knock at the door made her blood pump again.

"It's James. Let me in."

Kat whimpered in relief and flew to the door. She opened it just enough to admit him and slammed it closed. "Thank the Goddess!" she said, facing him in the flickering light of the single candle. It was only then she remembered she was half-dressed. James stared at her like a thirsty man at a glass of cold ale.

"Oh!" She took her bag from him and held it to her chest. His heated gaze swept over her, leaving her feeling naked. Heat pooled between her legs and her nipples tightened. She couldn't think of anything to say, so withdrew her hairbrush and sat on the end of the bed. She pulled the brush through her hair in long, soothing strokes, counting as she went.

"We should discuss sleeping arrangements." His voice sounded shaky, not his usual controlled self.

She drew a deep breath. "I hope you don't think less of me because I want you with me tonight. Those men looked at me as though they wished to ...Well, you know."

"You're a..." He cleared his throat. "You're a beautiful woman. What man wouldn't want to, ah, spend time with you?"

Kat swiveled to face him. "You." His eyes dropped to her breasts and she realized the candle sat behind her. He could probably see her shape beneath the thin fabric of her chemise.

He took a step forward, and his Adam's apple bobbed once, twice. "I'm not unmoved in your presence, Katrine. You shine like a beacon wherever you go. I'd be stone not to notice and want you."

He took another step toward her, yet it seemed to her as if he moved against his will. Of course it was against his will! She was nothing to him but a nuisance - a trap into which he had fallen and from which he must now extricate himself.

But his words traveled straight to her core, made her want things she had never yearned for. Like a man's strong arms around her, his lips on hers, his hard body pounding into her soft core. Kat almost blushed to admit it. Perhaps she could entice James to have his way with her this night and help her forget her melancholy.

She stood, placed the brush on the bed, and turned to him. Gathering her hair, she tossed it over her shoulder. He followed the movement of her breasts as if mesmerized. This strong, uptight, proper businessman was in her thrall! Kat had never held such power, but should she act on it? Could this be the night she lost her virginity and moved into womanhood? Would that be enough for her with James? Of course it would, it must be.

He took a step toward her and then another until she could have reached out and touched him if she desired. However, she instinctively knew James must make the first move. He caressed her cheek with the back of his fingers, sliding them down to her throat where her pulse pounded like a mountain stream in full flood! Heavens, her head felt like it could float away, yet he had barely touched her.

Kat took his wrist and steered his hand from her throat to the side of her breast, the quick gasp from James confirming he was entranced. His hand continued its downward slide to her waist, and he tugged her against him.

"Oh!" She couldn't help the whoosh of breath that escaped at the feel of him against her. She was almost naked, and his breeches were so fitted she felt every last hard inch of him. Kat looked up into eyes black with desire. Her arms crept around his neck and into his hair. His eyes slipped closed at the caress.

She kissed her way along his jawline to his ear and gave it a nip. His control seemed to snap. He let go of her waist and seized her face, his lips branding hers with a fierce kiss that didn't speak of control but of abandon and reckless desire. Too soon, he tore his lips away and peppered her neck and shoulders with frenzied kisses that drove her wild. Kat whimpered, desperate to be close with him, to be one with him. Everything within her strained to give itself to this man.

He devoured her with his eyes as he undid the buttons of her chemise and drew it off her shoulders. He slid his hands down the sides of her breasts and then upward to rub his thumbs over nipples made hard with longing. Each movement he made screamed of his experience and she almost lost her nerve. What did she know about the act of coupling, and how could she ever satisfy him?

James scooped her up and laid her on the bed, climbing over her, his mouth descending to her throat. Short stubble sent shivers coursing down her body, and she arched against him. Her fingers seemed to move of their own volition, down his shirt, unbuttoning it, and pulling it from his breeches. Her exploration came to an abrupt halt when his lips landed on her nipple, suckling and flicking the hard nub until Kat discerned a rising pressure in her core. He moved to the other breast, and she thought she might die of pleasure.

She could barely concentrate on him she was so taken over with his attentions. He seemed to be everywhere, and then his fingers landed on her waist and began sliding her pantaloons down. Kat groaned and bucked her hips off the bed. In seconds, she was unclothed and lay before his ravenous gaze. He nudged her legs apart and looked at the place that throbbed for him.

"James," she gasped. "I want…"

His greedy eyes caught hers, and she tingled all over at the longing in them. "I worship you, Katrine. You have the body of a goddess."

"Please…" She couldn't articulate her desire, so desperate was she for completion. If he touched her she would explode. And she didn't care what came after.

He pushed her legs wider and leaned in to kiss her in that most secret place which, until now, had been hers alone. His questing tongue found a hard nub and flicked it, sending her even higher - so much higher than she could ever have imagined. The pleasure and pressure within her mounted to almost painful heights then James inserted two fingers into her, and his lips encased her nipple.

Kat was lost. Her body exploded. Her mind burst with a thousand tiny pinpoints of light. She forgot where she was, forgot herself in the delight of completion. She came to a while later, and his lips were on her neck, his tongue drawing a line along her jaw. Kat turned to him, and their mouths met in a fury of kisses that made her press against him, wanting all he was able to offer. She pushed his shirt from broad shoulders, and her hands traced each muscle, every hard line and valley. He arched over her, and she pushed his breeches down, freeing him. He was magnificent. And large enough to make her pause.

Kat placed her hand around him, marveling at the contrast of hard strength and soft suppleness. A bead of moisture gathered at the tip, and she licked it off. He drew a ragged breath, his eyes revealing a desperation that surprised her.

"You like?" she asked, licking him again.

"You'll never know how much."

As she watched, horror replaced desire. "What's wrong?"

"We should stop." He slid off the bed. "This is no way to treat a lady."

Kat scrambled to the edge of the bed on her hands and knees. "What? Come back here and make love to me. We're only half finished!"

He stood with his back to her. "It would be taking advantage. Please, put your clothes on."

Kat got off the bed and walked up behind him. She gripped his waist and rained kisses down his spine all the way to the globes of his backside. He groaned.

"Don't tempt me. I'm trying to be a gentleman."

"I don't need you to be a gentleman right now. I need you to take me back to bed and take me to heaven again." Desperation had her in its grip and nothing mattered but the man before her. She laid her face against his back and breathed him in - clean sweat, musk and cloves. She would forever associate these scents with James, no matter what occurred between them.

He turned, gripped her forearms, and kissed her. Kat clung to him, praying it meant he had changed his mind. But, too soon, his lips were gone, and he was collecting his clothes. She stood, arms wrapped around herself, her gaze upon him, memorizing every small detail. She was still standing thus when he finished dressing.

"For the sake of the Goddess, woman," he snapped, "put some damned clothes on. Do you think I'm made of stone?" He gathered up her undergarments and threw them at her. They slipped to the floorboards.

"I don't understand what just happened." It was hard to be wrenched from a dream into cold reality. "Make me understand."

He deliberately turned his back on her again. "I have no right to be engaging in sexual pursuits with you. It isn't fair when we can never be more than a brief affair. Even that would be wrong."

"How can this be wrong? We're both unattached - aren't we? I realize you haven't come, but I'd be happy to oblige, whatever way you desire."

His head dropped. "Just take my word that this flirtation is not sensible. And I'm putting an end to it before I hurt you."

She placed herself before him, but he growled and began dressing her. She batted his hands away. "Look at me, damn you!"

His eyes roamed her body, and Kat tingled all over. He wanted her; she saw it in his eyes. "Take me, James."

For a long, tortured moment, she thought she had won, but he turned and headed to the door. "Get dressed. I'll wait in the hall."

CHAPTER 8

JAMES'S head ached from lack of sleep and not a small amount of sexual frustration. On his return to Katrine's room last night, she'd been in bed, thank the Goddess. Her back was turned to him, and she stayed that way. He made himself a bed on the floor just inside the door, stealing a pillow from the bed and wrapping himself in a spare blanket.

However, sleep was another matter. Each time he closed his eyes he saw her - bare, writhing with desire and fulfilment. He could no longer look upon Katrine without seeing her prone on that bed, naked, her black hair splayed over the white sheets and her nipples rosy from his attention. She was every man's fantasy, and he wanted her more than he'd ever wanted anything.

He shifted on the seat of the dray, trying to find a comfortable spot for the permanent erection he seemed to have these days. Soon they would stop for the midday meal, and he'd have to speak to her. They needed to talk, but could he settle things with Katrine without revealing his deep attraction to her? Perhaps if he could, she'd accept last evening as a pleasant interlude that should never be repeated.

He spied a sheltered spot and pulled the wagon into it, then fed the horse. Katrine dismounted and rubbed her stallion down, then went in search of water. One of the guards followed to ensure her safety, and they returned carrying two water bags. Once their mounts were watered, James took a seat next to Katrine.

"We're making good time," he said. "Two more nights and we'll be in Brightcastle."

"I, for one, can't wait," she muttered, her tone bitter.

"I'm sorry."

She laughed, the sound harsh. "Now you're sorry." Her voice dropped to a whisper. "We could've had a glorious night and instead you poisoned it. Why?"

"Just take my word for it. We can never be lovers."

She frowned at him. "Why not? Unless you are not attracted to me."

Now it was his turn to laugh. "That's not the problem."

"Then what? Are you married?"

James's gut gave a guilty heave. "Who would have me? A reclusive jeweler who is hardly ever home?" His personal life was none of her business. Last night's indiscretion would hurt no one as long as it didn't go any further.

She shook her head. "*I* would have you, indeed, I almost did last night. Tell me you didn't dream of me."

He couldn't answer without encouraging her. "Forget me. Our attraction to each other isn't meant to be."

"It's the witchcraft! Isn't it? I disgust you, and no respectable businessman would tie himself to a sorceress for even one night."

She had offered him an out, and, no matter how much it would hurt her, he had to take it unless he wished to tell the truth. Perhaps this was the lesser of two evils?

"I don't wish to be linked with magic, however beautiful and desirable you are." It was the truth. Any connection with sorcery might ruin him in business. The king had declared all magic practitioners be arrested. He risked everything associating with this woman. She didn't have to know the real reason he had stopped last night. To reveal the truth would be to expose himself as the worst hypocrite and risk all his carefully laid plans.

Her body stiffened at his words. "I see." She stood. "Then let's get back on the road and finish this association as swiftly as possible."

* * *

Kat didn't speak to James for the remainder of the day. The afternoon journey was uneventful, and the horror of the night hounds faded as if it was just a bad dream - as had her encounter with James. Of course, it had been glorious at the time, but he had tarnished it with his declaration earlier in the day.

She should've kept her distance, as her mind urged her to, but it was so hard to ignore the sexual attraction that zapped between them. She sighed. Distance from him would see her life return to normal, and, at least, she hadn't given herself to him. *That* would have been too much to bear - for her first coupling to be tarnished by his rejection of her sorcery.

Nearing sunset, they turned off the road and made camp in a clearing surrounded by tall fir trees. A nearby stream provided water, and the horses were soon fed. Kat lay dozing by the fire, her head propped on her saddle and her thoughts naturally drifting to last night's lovemaking. Her cheeks grew hot remembering what she had allowed James to do; remembering what she had wanted to do to him. She stood and took a bowl of steaming rabbit stew from the guard who was cooking dinner.

She glanced over at James, only to find his attention on the trees.

"Did you hear something?" she asked.

"I thought I did," he replied. "There was rustling in the undergrowth. Might be a small animal." He took his plate too and began eating.

The stew was just what Kat craved after a long day of travel. She enjoyed every spoonful and partook of a small glass of claret. It might calm her nerves. *I never used to be this jumpy!* A wolf howled, and the hair stood on the back of her neck. Her eyes snapped to James.

"We have nothing to fear from wolves, Katrine."

"I hope it's only a lone wolf out on a hunt and not a pack intent on man for dinner," she said, pulling her cloak closer. She finished her wine and stood, stretching the kinks from her spine. She moved to the dray and rolled out her bedding. Might James insist on sleeping with her tonight? Was that what she wanted, or would it be sweet torture? She placed her bed to one side of the dray so it would be his choice if he joined her or not, all the while shaking her head at being such a ninny.

"Katrine!" James's low growl brought her out of her musing, but he wasn't looking at her. His eyes flicked around the campsite at the trees bordering it. A chill settled in her stomach as she followed his gaze. Three night hounds stared at them from the northern side of the clearing and another four stood on the western side. *How many others are there?* Kat drew on her magic, ready to blast the beasts if necessary, while James pulled a knife from his boot, and the two guards drew arrows to their cheeks.

"Stay in the wagon!" James snapped, as the first hound stepped into the clearing. Two arrows struck it in the heart, but it still bounded three yards before falling. The death of one of their number appeared to be a sign for the others to attack, and all six remaining hounds flew at James and the guards.

James dragged a burning brand from the campfire and brandished it at two of the dogs while one of the guards did the same. The hounds were now too close to fire arrows. The scrape of short swords being drawn from scabbards cut through Kat as she tried to get a clear shot at one of the hounds. They had backed the men up against the dray.

A noise made her glance over her shoulder. A monstrous beast hurtled through the air toward her. "Watch your backs!" she cried, ducking.

The hound flew over her head and into the back of one of the guards, pushing him to his knees. But she didn't have time to worry about the men as she faced her own battle. Two more hounds stood in the trees on her side of the clearing, slavering, their blood red eyes fixed on her. As fear solid as a wall hit her, Kat drew on her power and sent two fireballs in quick succession, one to each of the hounds. One hit and the beast screamed and threw itself to the ground, writhing and howling. The other fireball missed its target.

"Damn you, I'm not going to die like this!" she screamed at the remaining beast. It froze as though listening to her words. Then it yapped twice and melted back into the forest.

She turned to check on James. He stood panting over the body of the huge beast that had leaped over her, while one of the guards held the bloodied neck of the other man. Another hound lay dead before them, making three killed by the men and one by her. The other beasts were gone. She scrambled down off the wagon and ran to James and the others.

Kat grasped James's forearms, desperate to ensure he had suffered no injury. He jerked away.

"I'm unhurt, Lady," he said. "See to Kova."

Kat withdrew, his snub hurting more than it should. She turned to the others. Kova, the injured guard, had a deep laceration to the back of his neck that required stitches. Dael, the other guard, was white with shock. "James, get Dael a drink while I tend to this wound." He could damn well make himself useful if he didn't need her.

She fetched her sewing kit and potions, cleaning the wound, and placing neat stitches to draw the edges together. All the while, Kat imbued her work with spells to aid healing and prevent the wound going foul. It was a serious injury and could yet take Kova's life. When she finished, she mixed the guard a potion for the pain.

By the time she finished, Kat was so exhausted she imagined a dark-cloaked man standing on the western edge of the clearing. She yelped in fright and rubbed her eyes. He was still there.

"James!" she hissed. "We have more company."

* * *

James stood as the tall stranger stepped into the clearing. His face was all straight lines and hard planes, and his green eyes contained prominent gold flecks. Long black hair lay over his shoulders and was restrained at his temples by a leather band worked with silver. He was dressed all in black and carried a long bow and a sword in a scabbard. Menace oozed from the man. James prepared to battle this new enemy, his hand closing around the knife in his boot.

"Don't think to fight me," the stranger growled.

The hair stood on James's neck at the timbre of his voice. "Who are you and what do you want?" he demanded as the man stepped closer

"You may call me Anton." The stranger's eyes swept the clearing. James got the impression he missed nothing - not the dead hounds, the injured guard, and, especially, not Katrine. He seemed most interested in *her*.

"My Lady," he said, sweeping a bow.

Katrine opened her mouth, but no words came out.

"You've had trouble," Anton said.

"We did." James replied for the speechless Katrine. He considered how much he should reveal to this man who had arrived immediately after the night hounds. The way he carried himself and his weapons spoke of an ability to handle any foe who came against him.

He walked around the camp, examining each dead animal. "Night hounds," he said. "A beast of legend. How come they to be hunting you?" Again, his gaze rested upon Katrine.

"We were in the wrong place at the wrong time," she said, staring at Anton as if he were a venomous snake.

He approached her, looking deep into her eyes for a long moment. James's hackles rose and he knew a desperate need to protect her - to place himself between Katrine and any danger.

"Those hounds," Anton said, "are hunters. They're drawn to their quarry." He looked at each of them in turn. "And so, I ask again, why were they hunting you?"

"They've been on our tail since we left Costa," James said, moving closer to Katrine.

"Did you chase them away?" Katrine asked Anton.

She looked almost desperate as she stared at their dark visitor. Perhaps she feared her magic had been revealed, both to the guards and to Anton. He was hardly likely to miss the charred remains of the beast blasted with Katrine's fireball.

"The hounds avoid me so perhaps they sensed my approach," Anton said. "Might I join you?"

Katrine looked to James. "Ah…that is…"

James studied their guest once again. Did they have any choice? He appeared more than capable of defeating all of them single-handed. Best to keep him close until they decided if they could trust him.

"You're welcome to share our fire," he said, gesturing for Anton to take a seat.

He smirked as though he knew exactly where James's thoughts lay. "That's very kind of you." He squatted before Kova and placed his hand on the man's forehead. "It's bad but I think he'll live."

"Are you a healer?" Katrine asked, her eyes narrowed.

"Let's just say I've seen many wounds," Anton replied. "You get to know which ones will turn bad."

James spooned stew from the pot into a bowl and offered it to their guest. He joined Anton by the fire while Katrine checked her patient.

"I'm James Tomel and this is Lady Aranati. If you were indeed responsible for the departure of the hounds, we're in your debt."

Anton shook James's hand and nodded to Katrine. "The roads are dangerous these days. You would do well to travel with more guards."

"We can do without your suggestions," Katrine said, eyes flashing, "and I'm capable of assessing my own patient, thank you."

James stood and drew Katrine over to the dray where they wouldn't be overheard. "What do you think you're doing? Don't antagonize him. We may need him yet."

"How do we know he didn't send those hounds?" she hissed, the shadows beneath her eyes like bruises. "He could be the one hunting us."

"It does seem very interesting that he should arrive in the midst of an attack," he said. "Regardless, we must be cautious until we decide what he wants." He wiped a hand across his brow. "Just let me do the talking." He returned to the fire, Katrine trailing, and poured wine for them all.

"What brings you to these parts?" James asked, stretching his legs before him.

"You have no cause to fear me. I have no interest in any of you." Anton fell silent and the only sound was the crackling of the fire. Perhaps he pondered how much to tell strangers he had met on the road. "I'm on a mission, sent by the king."

"Mission?" James asked.

"I'm not at liberty to reveal more than that to strangers." Anton looked at Katrine. "Suffice to say I'm no threat to you – unless you mean harm to the kingdom."

James frowned. The king's man in a land where magic was frowned upon could definitely spell trouble for them. But there was something about Anton's eyes that triggered a memory in James – an echo of a story from his childhood.

"We mean no harm," Katrine said. "I'm traveling to Brightcastle to see a friend. She's very sick."

"Ah, Brightcastle," Anton said, his face tightening into a grimace. "I've just spent some time there but would be happy to escort you safely to the city. If I'm welcome."

James looked to Katrine who shrugged her shoulders. Could they trust this man? He would be another hand to wield a sword if needed.

"If you can guarantee those beasts don't attack us again, you may join us." James said, holding out his hand.

This time, Anton offered the warrior's grip and James returned in kind, impressed by the strength revealed in the gesture. It was clear this man wouldn't be easily vanquished, and James fervently hoped he could be trusted.

"If you don't mind, I'll sleep now," Anton said. With those words, he rolled himself in a blanket near the injured guard and closed his eyes.

By all means, I'll take the first watch! Although the man's haughty words angered James, he hardly wanted the newcomer keeping watch over them when questions remained over his connection with the hounds. He arranged for Dael to relieve him in four hours, wished Katrine good night and began his vigil.

CHAPTER 9

AT dawn, Kat rose to tend Kova, the guard whose neck was injured. She had hardly slept for worrying about his condition, not to mention Anton and the hounds. She found Kova seated before the fire with Dael, a blanket around his shoulders. Of Anton and James, there was no sign.

"Good morning, Dael," she said. "How do you feel, Kova?"

"Terrible, Lady, but I'm alive, and I have you to thank for that."

"I'm glad I was able to help. I'll fix another drink for your pain."

She mixed herbs from her satchel, infusing the drink with healing magic as she stirred, then handed it to Kova.

"Where are the others?" she asked.

"Dealing with the bodies of the hounds, Lady," Kova said.

Kat didn't know if leaving the two men alone was a good idea. They reminded her of two tom cats circling each other, each waiting for the other to make the first attack. She was about to go looking for them when they walked back into camp.

"Is something amiss?" she asked, when she saw their grim faces.

"It's those hounds," James said. "We had a difficult time dealing with the bodies."

"You dragged them away?"

"We did, and they had already started to decompose," James said. "I've never seen anything like it. It's like nature wanted to get rid of the unholy things."

"Perhaps it did." Anton said, sniffing the pot of porridge. "Breakfast looks ready. Might I suggest we eat and get on the road as soon as we can?"

Kat shuddered at the thought of yet another bowl of gruel but smiled at Dael when he handed hers over. James took his breakfast in silence, casting wary glances at Anton. She sighed. *Just what we need, more tension.* After the meal, she went to the dray, rolled up her sleeping kit, and brushed her hair, wrapping it in a heavy shawl. It was getting colder as they moved further west, but tomorrow she would see Hetty. She sent a prayer to the Goddess that her mentor was still alive.

They broke camp and rejoined the road heading west, Kat riding on Demon alongside the dray. She had no chance to discuss the mysterious Anton with James, as Kova lay in the wagon behind him. Along with that, Anton had angled all morning for time alone with her, so she stuck close to James even if she couldn't speak with him on any meaningful topic.

Their new companion made her nervous; with good reason if night hounds feared him. She wasn't really scared of him, but a sixth sense told her he could be dangerous. She must discover if he posed a threat or not. Would he leave her alone when they reached their destination? And why had he really agreed to escort them? He had already visited Brightcastle; why retrace his steps?Distracted by musing on these questions, she fell behind the wagon without realizing, and Anton appeared at her side.

"Nice beast you ride, Lady."

She jumped at his deep voice so close. Meeting his gaze, she was trapped by the gold flecks she found there. "Demon is battle-trained," she said patting her mount's shoulder. "I'd trust him with my life."

"You may have to if you fall too far back."

Irritation swept through her. "I can look after myself, Sir!"

"Yes, I've a feeling you can. You would've vanquished those hounds if I hadn't happened along."

Kat stared straight ahead. His eyes saw too much. "Perhaps."

"One of them was burned, and he was the furthest from the fire. How do you explain it?"

"I don't need to explain anything to you. It's none of your concern. *You* didn't explain why night hounds avoid *you*."

"Touché, Lady."

She hid her smile. He was polished, this man, despite his hard exterior. It made him intriguing. James looked over his shoulder at them, and she met his troubled gaze.

"Well?" she asked Anton. "What *is* it about you that chases the hounds away?"

His chiseled face cracked a smile. "Persistent, aren't you?"

She fixed him with what she hoped was an unflinching stare. She wasn't afraid of him. She wasn't…

He huffed out a breath. "Let's say I have a little of the wolf about me, and the hounds sense it. I heard them hunting near the road, and I feared travelers might be in danger."

Kat decided to confront him. "The gold in your eyes, Anton. What does it mean?"

He frowned at her as if he didn't expect her to be so forward. "I'll tell you my story if you'll tell me yours."

Kat couldn't help the small shake of her head.

"I didn't think you would," he said. "But it's of no concern. There's plenty of time for you to change your mind. If you wish to talk, let me know." He cantered ahead, overtaking the dray, his eyes searching the trees.

Kat rode up alongside James again.

"What have you been telling him, Katrine?"

"Nothing," she snapped. "But I reserve the right to tell him anything I wish."

"Is that wise?"

"I'll decide when the time comes. He claims he has something of the wolf about him, and that's why the hounds ran off."

"What does he mean by that?" He worked his shoulders and neck.

"Who can tell? But I believe we *do* have him to thank for chasing the hounds away last night."

She stared at Anton's back. He rode a horse like he'd been born on one, his weapons arrayed about him. She guessed he wouldn't be hampered by his armory.

James shook his head. "We can't trust him."

"Did I say I trusted him?"

"If you take my advice, you'll accept his help to get to Brightcastle and say nothing of yourself."

She leaned closer. "I asked about his eyes," she whispered. "They're similar to mine. I'm curious." She couldn't help wondering if Anton held magic of his own, and, if so, what it was. Would he keep to his pledge and reveal his secrets if she told him hers? *Was* he trustworthy? Or was James right?

Kat watched the enigmatic Anton for the remainder of the day, determined to discover more about their companion. Bird song died as he approached, and Dael, their one remaining able-bodied guard, avoided the man. Anton's own horse appeared wary, rolling its eyes and shivering when he patted it. The dun stallion seemed otherwise unflappable, so it was surprising it should fear its rider.

Anton himself rode wrapped in his thoughts, it seemed, and he intermittently left the road, entering the trees. He would be gone for a half hour then return, sometimes from behind them. It was all very mysterious.

As Kat grew increasingly intrigued and concerned, she resolved to uncover who – or *what* – Anton was.

At dusk, they drew off the road into a clearing and prepared their camp. Anton rubbed down his horse and announced he'd fetch their supper. He left with his bow and returned a short time later with four large hares. He proceeded to skin them, and they were soon roasting over the fire.

Kat couldn't take her eyes from him. It seemed James had noticed.

He blocked her line of sight to Anton and drew her gaze. "You don't have to stare at the man!" he hissed.

"I wasn't aware I was," she lied. "Doesn't he intrigue you?"

"Not for the same reasons he interests you, I suspect," he snapped.

Kat's palm itched to slap the haughty jeweler on the face, but she clenched her fist against her thigh instead. "Don't be coarse. And keep your voice down. He has exceptional hearing."

James shook his head. "My, my, you *have* been watching closely."

"Yes, I have, and it would be a mighty good idea for you to be observant too." She led him further from the others. "I intend to find out who and what Anton is. The more we know, the safer we'll be."

"I see what he is, Katrine. He's an outlaw. And I *have* been watching – closely. I've seen the way Dael avoids him. And his horse fears him. He beats the poor animal!"

She frowned. "I haven't seen evidence of cruelty. Did you see the way he tended to his dun before fetching supper? And his hunting prowess is second to none! Could you fetch four hares in that short time?"

"I want you to stay away from him," he said. "It's the only way I can ensure your safety."

She raised her hand, but only to pat his cheek. He was so handsome when he scowled at her. "Don't worry, James. I'll be careful."

However, Kat wasn't as unconcerned about their companion as she wanted James to think. Anton was mysterious, with an element of menace she had not seen in other men. She didn't wish to place herself under his scrutiny by revealing her secrets. However, he already suspected her of having magic talents, and, if he too harbored secrets, where was the risk?

She sat on a log near the fire, her eyes fixed on the snapping flames, while she pondered what to do. Hetty had never told her anything that covered this situation. She wondered again if her friend was still alive, if she would be too late.

"What upsets you?" Anton's deep voice drew her from her reverie, and she wiped away a tear. She took a deep breath and addressed him.

"I'm concerned I'll be too late to help my friend."

His hooded eyes revealed nothing as he turned the hares. "Your friend and mentor?"

"Yes."

"Is her name Hetty, by any chance?"

Kat could not have been more shocked if he had stripped naked and run around their campsite. "You have discerned my secret." How could he have known? He knew Hetty, or of her, that was clear.

Anton stood. "The dinner will be a while yet. Please, join me on a walk. You'll be quite safe." He ghosted from the clearing, making scarcely a rustle of his cloak as he left.

Kat looked to James who shook his head. "Give me ten minutes. If I haven't returned, come looking." She hurried after Anton.

She found him leaning against a huge tree not far from the clearing. "You know my secret if you know Hetty."

"You're a witch?"

She nodded. "I've had the talent for years, but recently I had a magical experience. It left me changed, and that's where I got the sparkles in my eyes. How did you come by yours?"

"You're very direct."

"I find it saves time." She stared at Anton, willing him to reveal all his secrets.

"I was drawn to you and your party last night. My talent leads me to find those who are in need. I'm a Defender."

Kat searched her memory for clues as to what the word meant. *Shapeshifter?* "You can change your form."

"I have three animal forms – bear, wolf and hawk."

"Well that explains why the hounds fear you," Kat said. "And your horse, he doesn't like you either."

"It's a hard fear to overcome. I've accepted the fact that my mount will never love me." If the man felt sorrow, then Kat believed this hurt him.

"I could've dealt with the night hounds last night," she said, "but I try not to use my powers unless I have to, especially in public. This society isn't ready for the overt use of magic yet. Perhaps it never will be."

Anton nodded. "I've found that to be so. Indeed, your mentor hides herself within the community. Regardless, Hetty has been a supporter of mine in the past." He looked as though he wanted to say more. How intriguing!

It was also an interesting coincidence that this man should arrive now, and they should both know Hetty. What did it all mean?

Someone cleared their throat behind her. She turned to find James standing there.

"Dinner is ready," he said, his gaze fixed on Anton. The two men stared at each other, like wary wolves, each waiting for the other to strike or back down. She placed her hand on James's shoulder, and his eyes, full of anger, locked on hers. Then he turned and strode back to their camp. Was he angry with her or Anton and why?

Kat wandered back in her own time and took her share of the meat and a piece of bread. She sat on a log near the fire and the others did the same, each keeping company with their own thoughts. After the meal, Dael patrolled the perimeter. The silence grew oppressive as Kat chose and discarded topic after topic. The men didn't seem to care.

"Anton," she said, finally. "What will you do when we reach Brightcastle tomorrow?"

"I'll leave you."

"Where will you go?" she asked.

"I…I may visit someone in the city, since I'm close again." He raked his fingers across his chin. "Then I'm bound for Wildecoast."

"This person you wish to visit," Kat said. "Is it a woman?"

Anton frowned so deeply, Kat held her breath. Had she asked one question too many?

James stood abruptly, and his plate slid into the dirt. "*I* know who you will visit. I've been trying to puzzle out who you are. Your name rang a bell, just not the right one. You're *Vard* Anton, once captain in Brightcastle. You abducted Princess Alecia who has not long returned, a babe in arms. It doesn't take much intelligence to work out who the child's father is."

Kat studied Anton's face and saw many things including anger. What she hadn't expected was the sadness that settled on him like a heavy cloak. "It's none of your concern. Princess Alecia has returned to her rightful home, and she is safe."

"Rumor is the king pardoned you," James ground out. "Is that all it is? Rumor?"

Vard rose slowly from his log. "I don't have the paper to prove it but yes, I'm a pardoned man. As I stated earlier, I'm on a mission from His Majesty."

Kat's heart pounded. Who did James think he was, challenging Anton like this?

"I'll see you pay for what you did, one way or another," James said, his hand moving to his sleeve and the knife Kat knew was hidden there. She leaped toward him and seized his hand before he drew the blade.

"Are you insane?" she hissed. "He'll gut you like a fish. This isn't the way."

His grey eyes met hers. He was unafraid. What kind of craftsman wasn't fearful of a man of Vard Anton's ability? His story and the princess's were legend. If only half of it was true, he was, indeed, a formidable foe.

"He has you under his spell, and he's dangerous. Look what he did to the princess. Her life is ruined!" James stood before her, his fists clenched, fire blazing from his eyes.

Kat glanced behind her and found Anton poised on the balls of his feet, but no weapon was in sight. She turned to James. "Back off. You don't want this confrontation." She took a step toward him which forced him out of the fire circle and away from danger. She kept walking until he refused to back up any further. "What's wrong with you?" she asked.

His jaw clenched, and he closed his eyes as if getting his anger under control was a monumental effort. "You're right." He stalked off across the camp and into the trees.

She stared after him, uncertain if she should follow. In the end, she wandered after him and found him with his forehead against the smooth bark of a silver birch. She placed her hand on his shoulder.

"What has you so agitated?"

"I'd rather not talk about it."

"Look at me," she said.

With great reluctance it seemed, he turned to face her. His throat bobbed in a swallow, and he heaved a great breath. Since their interlude of two nights ago, James had retreated into his shell, and she didn't understand why. Wasn't it natural to have sexual partners when you were a virile man?

And yet something had stopped him from completing the act with her. He said it was her magic but something about that didn't ring true. What else could it be? He even admitted being attracted to her.

"Has this mood of yours got anything to do with us?" she asked

He huffed out a breath. "Katrine! There is no *us*! I'm sorry I took liberties the other night. Put it down to tiredness and the strange things that have happened lately. Danger has a way of loosening the restraints a man habitually applies to his behaviour."

"Really? You're sorry?" She reefed her fingers through her hair, and his eyes followed her violet nails. "It was glorious, and, when you apologize, I feel as though what we did was wrong."

"Of course, it's wrong!" he snapped. "I shouldn't be having these feelings."

"What feelings? Desire? Excitement?" She stepped closer, and his body tensed. She took another step, so they were toe to toe, and stared up into his face.

"Katrine…"

She wrapped her arms around his neck, her lips so close to his she could feel his ragged breath. "I wish to experience what it's like to bed a man, and I've chosen you."

He clutched her arms, and she chose that moment to kiss him, to take what she wanted. As he gasped with surprise, Kat invaded his mouth, deepening the kiss, desperate to leave him in no doubt of her feelings.

At first his hands tightened, and she feared he'd pull her arms from around his neck, but, in the end, his hands slid to her waist. Crushing her body against his, he mastered her in every way, with his lips, his hands and his body. She gloried in the thrust of his tongue as it danced with hers, in the slide of his long fingers through her hair and in the hard strength pitted against her desire.

He grasped her hair and pulled her head back, exposing her neck, and nibbled his way down to her collar bone, stopping to undo several buttons. She gasped as his tongue slid across the swell of her breast, and she nudged her body against the bulge in his breeches. He wanted her, she was in no doubt of it. Could she convince him to put his reservations aside and find his completion in her?

Her hips drove at him, desperate to show she was ready to receive him. The only thing that held her up was the tight band of his arm across her back. She combed her nails through his hair, welding his lips to her breasts, and when his thigh nudged between her legs she nearly exploded. The shock of it all had her gasping for breath.

But when she expected to feel his hands on the fastening of her breeches, James pulled his mouth from her skin. His grey eyes found a stray beam of moonlight and she observed his dawning awareness. He drew back, waiting for her to take her weight before removing his arm, his gaze on her heaving chest.

It was all Kat could do to breathe, let alone process what had occurred between them. She was in a state, her mind scrambled by his loving, and her body still yearning for its promised union with this man.

"You can't pull away again," she snapped. "I want this over, now!"

"Keep your voice down and cover yourself." He stepped toward her and drew the edges of her tunic together. "Please."

She closed her eyes and drew a ragged breath then buttoned her tunic. "Don't you sense it, James?" He turned side on. His striking profile mocked her. "There's attraction between us. You can't deny it. Sooner or later you'll come to me, and we'll be one. Why can't that moment be now?"

His eyes snapped to hers. "We aren't animals. I won't deny I'm attracted to you, but there's nothing inevitable about it. And to do this here and now with Anton and the others mere yards away?" He huffed a great breath and his eyes narrowed. "You need to understand that, when we reach Brightcastle, I'll never see you again."

He brushed past her, long strides taking him back to the clearing. Kat slumped onto a nearby rock, fighting back stupid tears. Why must her body drive her toward this man who refused to give in to what they both wanted? She straightened her tunic and dried her eyes so she could return to the camp with dignity. James had his own reasons for spurning her, but she'd not give up on him just yet.

CHAPTER 10

A TENSE day followed the strained night. Nobody had spoken up to bedtime the previous evening except to organize a watch to be kept. James shared the duty, having taken the middle shift. The shadows under his eyes made him more handsome to Kat, adding an air of mystery that almost rivalled Vard Anton's. The Defender kept to himself, riding ahead and out of sight, except for the stop at midday.

Kat had tried to converse with James several times, but he offered only one syllable answers which left her in no doubt that the sooner they parted company the better. Kova was now recovered enough to ride his horse and keep Dael company, but privacy hadn't encouraged James to make any sort of conversation with her.

By the time Vard approached midafternoon to announce he had spotted the towers of the Brightcastle Keep, Kat's nerves were wound tighter than the strings of a fiddle. Her horse pranced and threw his head so much she spent most of the time trying to control him and the rest scanning the trees to ensure there were no surprises awaiting them.

"Loosen the reins, Lady," Vard said. "The poor beast will have a sore mouth if you keep yanking on him."

"I am *not* yanking," she said, through clenched teeth. "Are you sure nothing stalks us?"

"I'm sure. Your beast picks up on your nerves. Relax, and he'll be less anxious."

She scowled at him. As if anyone could relax in her situation. There was a pack of night hounds after her, a Defender who was once an outlaw in her party, and an insufferable companion who would not… Kat wasn't willing to put words to that situation. Perhaps she was wrong to hope for anything more with James?

Time to think of other issues. Unlike James, Kat had reserved her opinion of Vard's guilt in the matter of Princess Alecia's kidnapping. She had heard disturbing rumors of Prince Jiseve Zialni, Alecia's father. If they were true, and Hetty said they were, she understood why the princess had fled her home in the company of Vard Anton.

As to whether the two were a love match, Hetty again confirmed this, though it appeared there was trouble in paradise. Vard had a new life in Wildecoast, while the princess had returned to Brightcastle. And she had a child, a daughter, less than a year old. Was Vard the father as James had accused?

Kat longed to ask him, but her courage had failed her more than once, and Hetty had never mentioned the princess being with child on her previous visits. She chose to ask a more urgent question. "Will I have the hounds on my tail as soon as you leave, Anton?" He had asked her to preserve his cover in front of the guards.

"I urge caution, Lady," Vard said. "Brightcastle is a place of magic that will attract them, and I can't stay long. Ask Hetty how you can ward them off if she is well enough." With those words, Vard turned his horse and cantered ahead, his body moving as one with his mount.

If she is well enough. Kat's stomach clenched tighter than a clam, bringing her nerves back into full play. Demon tossed his head, and she was back where she began before Vard approached.

She calmed Demon and glanced across at James who had a deep scowl on his face.

"When we get to Brightcastle," he said, "I'm going to follow that man and keep an eye on him." His whole focus was on Vard as he cantered into the distance.

"Why?" she asked.

He jumped and looked across at Kat as though he was surprised he had spoken out loud.

"I want to know what he's up to."

"Surely it's none of your concern?"

"I'm making it my business. I don't trust him."

Kat sighed. "Please yourself," she said. "James…I wanted to thank you for helping me reach Brightcastle. It has been a dangerous journey. I regret the loss of your man and Kova's injury. It was good of you to place yourself at risk for me. I'm in your debt."

If anything, he frowned more deeply. "I wouldn't be much of a gentleman if I allowed a lady to travel alone. Anyone would have done the same."

"No, they wouldn't," she said. "Most would have said good riddance and had not a moment's regret. If there is ever anything I can do to repay you, please let me know."

"There's nothing owing, Katrine." His voice was abrupt. He may as well have said her chapter in his life was coming to an end and he welcomed it. If she owed him nothing, there was no reason for their paths to ever cross again. And yet Kat was sure she'd think of the jeweler long after he left her.

She nodded, and he went back to contemplating the road ahead. The rest of the journey was undertaken in silence with only the jingle of harness and the grinding of the wheels to relieve the monotony. Had there ever been a less united group of travelers? Kat bent her thoughts to Hetty and how surprised the old woman would be to see her.

They reached the outer city wall and passed through the gate. Vard lifted his hand in farewell and cantered his dun toward a side street, the hood of his cloak pulled low. Kat, James, and Kova continued up the main street while, at a nod from James, Dael followed Vard at a distance. Surely the Defender would spot Dael in an instant?

Once they reached a stable near Hetty's house, Kat reined in.

"I'll leave you now, James," she said. "Thanks once again."

James regarded her, his eyes inscrutable. "If you're sure you'll be safe, I bid you farewell. I hope your friend is soon well again." With those parting words, he rode on with Kova.

She watched as her companions disappeared. Certainly, James couldn't wait to be rid of her. Why did the Goddess bring such a man into her life only to allow her to lose him? A cold wind swirled and Kat shivered as she drew her cloak closer and went in search of a stall for her horse.

Kat stood before Hetty's door, her hand raised to knock, when the door swung open. She was confronted by a blonde woman about her own age, dressed in gray breeches and tunic. The blonde's astonished lilac eyes swept over Kat.

"Who are you?" the woman snapped.

Kat drew herself up at the tone of authority in the woman's voice. "Katrine Aranati. And your name is?"

"Alecia Zialni."

The princess!

She grasped Kat's arm and pulled her into the house, closing the door and leaning against it. "Hetty has mentioned you."

Kat could have said she had heard of Alecia, but it wouldn't hurt to keep the woman on the back foot. *As if she cares if you've heard of her or not, you twit. She'd assume you knew of her.* "How is Hetty?"

Alecia's eyes darted away, and a frown appeared on her brow. "I hate to say it, but she's very ill." She lowered her voice further. "I've known Hetty for years. She's never sick, and now nothing seems to make her better."

Kat turned and headed for the stairs which led to the bedrooms.

Alecia called her back. "I've made a pallet in the kitchen where it's warmer—"

Kat stopped in the doorway to the kitchen, her eyes drawn to the bed in the corner where Hetty lay, her breath rasping in and out of her body.

"Don't just stand there, girl," Hetty said. "Since you ignored my order to stay away, you'd best come closer. I won't bite."

She advanced, noting the greyish hue of Hetty's face and her bloodless lips. She had lost weight and now reminded Kat of a skeleton with skin stretched over the bones.

"Hetty!" Kat threw herself down on her knees and reached for the frail body of her friend, drawing her close, surprised when the skeletal arms latched onto her. Hetty never showed emotion.

When Kat drew back and settled Hetty against the pillows, a hacking cough wracked the old woman's fragile body. It continued until Kat feared it might be the end of her. She turned to Alecia. "What have you been doing for her?"

Alecia wrung her hands, tears in her eyes. "I've made her warm and fed her twice a day with chicken broth. It's the only thing she can swallow." The princess drew closer. "Her magic has failed, or she would've been able to make medicine to fix the cough."

Kat shivered at the fear in Alecia's eyes. She reached out and squeezed her hand. "I'm here to care for her now. I'll see all is done to help her recover."

Alecia nodded and closed her eyes, a tear escaping. "I…I need her, Katrine. She's all I have left from my childhood. Please don't fail her."

"I'll do all I can." Kat turned to the kitchen shelves and fetched the first ingredient for the potion.

It was midnight before Kat had a moment to herself. She sat before the kitchen fire, its crackling and the sleeping Hetty's harsh breathing the only sounds. Princess Alecia had left soon after Kat arrived, and she found herself craving company. A chill wind rattled the windows, and the cold settled in her gut too. Nothing had gone right from the time she left Esta, but she had made pilgrimages before and never found herself in strife. What had changed?

Everything. Her world was under siege from all directions. First her sister marrying, and then James and his damned determination to shut her out of his life. The night hounds had threatened her very existence, and now Hetty could die - was more than halfway there if Kat was any judge. She rubbed her arms, trying to understand why she was suddenly dealing with everything at once. Why wasn't she born a normal woman with no magic and no creatures on her tail?

And what was the reason for her existence? Esta didn't need her, for all her protestations. Kat believed things happened for a reason. Well, what was the reason for the Crystal Cave and her current condition?

She threw another log on the fire and drew a blanket around her, desperate to get warm. Perhaps another cup of tea might do the trick? As Kat made her brew, she pondered her next move. The house was bare of food and medicines, but she had given Alecia a list of all she required. There was no need to leave the house.

Perhaps she should check on James, although she didn't know how to find him. And he wouldn't want to see her. Besides, she couldn't risk an encounter with the hounds. She sipped her tea and pared her thoughts back to the reason for being in Brightcastle. *Hetty.*

Kat needed to concentrate on getting Hetty well, then she could move forward with her own life. She rose from her chair and checked on the sleeping woman. Her breathing seemed easier, and she hadn't coughed for an hour. It must be a good sign. She placed her hand on Hetty's forehead and spoke the first words of another healing spell.

* * *

After a restless night, James joined his friend Cal, the master goldsmith, in the tiny kitchen of the residence behind his shop. He spooned porridge into his mouth as Cal related all the latest news from Brightcastle and beyond. However, his mind was only half on his friend. The remainder wondered how Katrine was and if she thought of him. He was an idiot, of course.

He had deliberately forced her from his mind these last two days in order to bring his world back on an even keel. He couldn't harbor feelings for her for many reasons.

It was better this way. He needed to be alone, unaffected by matters of the heart. Katrine could never discover his secrets, though she had revealed hers to him. She was a witch and the kingdom shunned her sort. But the thought of betraying her, as he should, pained him, so her secret would remain safe.

"Are you going to see her?" Cal asked.

The question jerked James from his musing, and, for a moment, he worried he had given himself away. Then he realized his friend was not talking about Katrine.

"Of course. My life wouldn't be worth living if I didn't," he replied.

Cal grinned. "There should be more reason than that to go calling. She's a fetching woman, despite her widow's weeds. How long has it been since her husband's death?"

"Almost two years." James pondered his betrothed's habitual black garb. He'd never seen her in anything else. He looked forward to her throwing off the damned black and putting on some color. She was, after all, still young and attractive, with the rest of her life ahead. "Can I get your man to deliver a letter to Lady Stenmore? My men are already out and about."

"Certainly. Pen it now, and I'll see it's delivered. In the meantime, I wondered how long you plan to stay."

"Until I complete my duties. I have meetings to attend, and I must see Princess Benae."

"And, of course, pay your respects to Lady Stenmore."

"I don't understand why you keep returning to her," James snapped. For some reason, it irritated him to think of his betrothed. It was stupid, of course. Melanis Stenmore was perfect for him - a young widow, sensible and intelligent, whose husband was a banker before his death. She would be a great asset for his business, and her contacts would prove invaluable. Most important of all, she was stable and predictable. An image of Katrine, long dark hair streaming behind her as she galloped her horse into him, forced its way into his consciousness. He shoved it back where it belonged.

Cal laughed. "You should let your hair down, James. Have a little fun. Life's too short to waste on work and boredom."

"I'll have you know my life has been anything but boring of late."

"Do tell!" Cal settled against the kitchen bench and poured himself another mug of tea. "I believe the master jeweler is blushing!"

He fixed Cal with a cold stare. "You wish. I refer to one of my traveling companions. I had the pleasure of Vard Anton's company for the last two days."

Cal whistled. "My, my, the elusive captain returns. Where is he now?"

James sighed. "I don't know where he went. I set Dael to follow him. That lasted all of an hour."

"Not surprising. The man is a legend. It's said he returned from insanity to find Princess Alecia. They were linked at one time. He was her protector."

James waved his hand. "I know all of that. And he's only a man. I didn't detect any madness while he was with us, although he did keep to himself."

"There are other rumors." His friend fixed him with a sly smile. "It's also said you entered Brightcastle with an attractive woman, wearing men's garb. Who is she?"

James stiffened. "Just a traveler we met on the road. No one you need to know about."

"You know better than that, James. Like you, I need to monitor any strangers in this city. If you won't tell me, I'll have to seek out the lass myself. I may even share a meal with her ..."

"Stay away from her," James snapped. *Damn, now he'll know she's someone of interest, at least to me.* "She's visiting a sick friend. Nothing to concern you."

"Mmm." Cal tapped his lips as he watched James. "I'll leave her alone for now, but she had better behave herself while in town."

James ground his teeth. Katrine would get herself into trouble the first time she left Hetty's house. His gut took a dive as his thoughts leaped to what trouble she might attract. Perhaps he'd watch her himself, or get Dael to do it. But what about when he left for Costa? She'd be on her own. And it was what he wanted, to be out of her life forever.

"Do what you must," James snapped. "You will anyway. I have people to meet." He pulled a sealed parchment from his pocket and handed it to Cal. "I'd appreciate it if you could send this note to Lady Stenmore."

"Certainly. Have a good day, and I'll meet you for dinner at our usual haunt."

James waved distractedly as he left the shop via the back alley, his thoughts already on those he needed to see while in the city. They were craftsmen from all the guilds in the city, and they formed his eyes and ears. He spent the morning collecting news from his network and, by luncheon, had a pocket of notes and a head full of information that required sifting through.

The next person on his list was Lady Stenmore. Her residence was the perfect place to sort through the mess of information he had gleaned. Luckily, he was only a short walk from her mansion, though luck had nothing to do with it.

He stepped through her front gate and across a paved courtyard to the steps and front door. As he raised his hand to knock, her porter opened the door and bowed.

"Lady Stenmore has been expecting you, Sir."

"Hello, Roth," he said. "How is her ladyship?"

"She is well, Sir," Roth said, and took James's cloak. "Please follow me to the drawing room."

The porter was full of airs and graces. James had never seen him smile in all the time he had known the man. He stepped through the door of the drawing room, and a beautiful blonde woman in a black satin gown stood to greet him. Melanis Stenmore.

"James," she said, embracing him and kissing both of his cheeks. "It's marvelous to see you." She turned to Roth. "Have luncheon served in here."

The servant left, and Melanis drew James to her, lips close to his ear. "I've missed you terribly. When are we to make our betrothal public, so I'll never be without you again?"

"You'd still be on your own when I traveled, Lady Stenmore," he replied, pulling away from her and crossing to the fireplace where a cheerful blaze warmed the room.

Not daunted by his words, she walked up behind him, and her arms circled his middle, her jasmine fragrance filling his nose. "So formal, darling. There's no one to hear." Her nails scored his chest, reminding him of Katrine's, and a kernel of passion stirred.

He snatched a breath and turned to her, pulling her against him and threading his fingers up into her hair. His lips crashed against hers, and, for a moment, he was lost in the sensual dance he'd come to expect with Melanis. But unease curled its way up from within, and, no matter how his body wished to fall into old habits, he pulled away. "I had work in mind. Can you help me sort through the information I received this morning?"

She pouted, and he reflected it looked silly on this elegant woman. "I don't *want* to work. Why would you suggest that when we've been apart for so long?"

Indeed, why? He didn't know himself. Every other visit he had paid to Melanis resulted in them ending up in bed together, though their betrothal was not yet official. Only this time, he had less desire to sample her delights - and they were many. Melanis knew how to pleasure a man. He often wondered how a lady had learned all the tricks in her repertoire. But where once a marriage to Lady Stenmore had appeared the ideal pathway to a life of comfort and predictability, now he wasn't sure.

"I have much on my mind, Melanis. Don't press me, or I'll find somewhere else to work."

Her eyes widened at his snappy retort. "You have tired of me."

"How can I have tired of you? I haven't seen you."

"They say absence makes the heart grow fonder, but I rather think it's the opposite." She folded her arms across her middle, and her pale blue eyes conveyed a world of hurt. "There's someone else. I know the signs."

He shook his head. "There is no one else." Hadn't he deliberately distanced himself from Katrine because of Melanis?

Roth arrived with luncheon which he set out on the sideboard. Neither of them spoke as the porter worked and then left. James poured a cup of tea and took his lunch over to a table by the window where he laid his notes in a pile. Melanis drifted after him.

"Aren't you going to eat?" he asked.

She shook her head. "I've lost my appetite. Pass me a pile, and I'll help." She bent her head over the papers, making brief notes in her neat script.

Within the hour, they had the information collated, and she sat back, watching as he folded the summaries and tucked them inside his shirt.

"What has happened, James?" she asked. "You've never been so cold toward me."

He stood, walked to the fireplace, and threw all the notes he had gleaned from his contacts that morning into the fire. It was no easy question his lady asked him. He turned to her.

"I admit I've been pondering the future," he said. "I wonder if it's fair to you to continue our betrothal."

Her eyes widened, her hands flying to her throat. She rose and paced across the room away from him, shoulders tight, her steps small and hurried. "I never thought to hear those words from you."

"I know it must be somewhat of a shock, my dear, but is a union with me truly what your heart desires?"

She spun to face him. "Yes! It's *all* I wish for. I dream of the children we'll have. The wedding plans are almost complete. I believed we were close to announcing our betrothal, and we could be wed in short order." She heaved a great breath, and he was appalled to see tears in her eyes. "We're an ideal match!"

"But do you love me?"

"Love! What's love when compared to the life we have planned?" She joined him at the fireplace and clasped his hands in hers, looking up at him with eyes he used to admire. "We'll be invincible as a team, James. We'll be wealthy and powerful, and all will seek our advice and company. How could you contemplate turning your back on me?"

Confusion roiled in his gut. The picture she painted was the life he had always craved when he escaped the farm. Only now it didn't sound as compelling as it once had. Could it be he now longed for something different? "I haven't decided anything, Melanis, however I think we should take our time - make sure it's what we both want."

She placed her hands on her hips. "It's only *you* who must decide. I'm ready to commit my life to you, have your children, and be your partner." She stepped back out of reach. "I don't wish to see you until you can tell me you're ready for our official announcement." Her head came up, and she was every bit the proud noblewoman.

"I expect to see you before you leave Brightcastle." She turned and left the room.

CHAPTER 11

KAT sat dozing in front of the fire in Hetty's kitchen, her daydreams full of James and the adventures they had shared. She idly wondered where he was and what he was doing. She hadn't set foot outside the house since she arrived, caring for Hetty for a full day and two nights. Only the visit yesterday of Princess Alecia, bearing medicines and food, had broken the monotony and the worry.

Hetty was a little better, but the nursing and spells should've had a greater effect. And Kat's magic waned as her exhaustion grew. She didn't know what else she could do.

Her stomach grumbled. She rose from the rocking chair, placed a pot of stew over the fire, and added wood. She stood by Hetty, watching the easier movements of the old woman's chest, but when she took in the pallor of her face and lips, her stomach fluttered with dread. Since their first conversation the day Kat arrived, Hetty had barely been conscious and had eaten only one bowl of watery broth. If she didn't awake soon, she would die of starvation.

Kat turned back to the fire and swapped the stew pot for the kettle. She had never drunk so many cups of tea or said so many prayers. If only she could be sure she was winning this fight. If only Hetty would wake up and snap at her. She longed to see the fire back in her friend's dark eyes.

As she was finishing breakfast, there was a knock at the door, and her heart started pounding. She hurried out and opened it, taking care to keep the magical shield in place.

"Good morning, Princess," she said, as Alecia brushed past dressed in grey breeches and tunic, a heavy forest green cape swirling around her legs.

"How is she?" Alecia was the only other person who cared if Hetty lived or died.

"Perhaps a little better."

Alecia paused to study Kat. "You look dreadful."

She pushed her hands through hair that hadn't seen a brush in over a day. "I'm tired, that's all. Please go through."

The princess frowned at her, then turned and headed into the kitchen. She stood gazing down at Hetty then faced Kat. "What else can be done?"

She shrugged her shoulders. "I can't think of anything. I've exhausted all my potions, spells, and charms, only to have this small improvement. Are you sure you know of no local wise woman we could call on?"

Alecia snorted. "Local wise woman, indeed. If *you* can't help, then such a woman will be useless. There's only one who might be able to aid us, and she has refused."

Kat's mouth dropped open. "Why? Who is she?"

"The woman who married my father!"

"Princess Benae?"

Alecia's eyes flashed fire. "She's no princess!"

Kat took a deep breath to control her temper. "Regardless, why did she refuse to aid you?"

Alecia wore such a fierce look Kat completely believed the stories of the princess protecting her people by fighting. "There's bad blood between Benae and Hetty, and neither of them will tell me why. Ramón knows, and, each time I reference it, he goes red in the face."

"Ramón? He's Steward of Brightcastle and Benae's husband, is he not?" Kat asked.

Again, Alecia snorted. "Steward of Brightcastle! My uncle the king must need his head read to place those two in charge of such an important region. I'm preparing to petition him. He must give this principality to me. *I* am the rightful heir. Let him tell me himself that being female means I can't inherit the throne."

Kat couldn't keep up with Alecia's rapid changes of direction. "Princess, what about Hetty? Can't you ask Benae again? Perhaps she has a potion she can prepare for us. She need not even see Hetty."

Alecia scowled, and Kat was tempted to take a step back, but she refused to allow this fierce woman to intimidate her.

"Her healing is not through potions, though she uses them to disguise what she is really doing. She must lay hands on her patient, but she won't leave the castle. She says she won't place her babe at risk." Alecia's face softened. "He's such a tiny mite and not robust."

"That's the reason she won't help? Fear for her child?"

"It's one of them. She does seem to hate Hetty, however, and I'd love to understand why."

"This is getting us nowhere!" Kat strode across the parlor and back again. "I can't stand this waiting."

Alecia stood watching her. "I thought I was the only one who cared for Hetty."

Kat stopped, hands on hips. "I care very much. When I realized she was ill, I left immediately, fearing I'd be too late."

"And you traveled alone?"

She felt her face heat. "No, I had an escort. I traveled with a respected citizen of Costa." Should she mention Vard Anton? She was curious to learn more of him and Alecia, and decided to chance it. "We met Vard Anton two days out from Brightcastle."

Alecia went perfectly still, and her face blanched. "You *did*?"

"Do you wish to hear how he is?"

The princess's eyes dropped to her hands which were clenched in front of her. "He and I recently spoke. He is on his own path for now and I'm on mine. I can't let him back into our lives until I'm sure it will be forever."

"Then you still love him?"

103

Alecia's fiery gaze returned. "It's none of your concern. Iona and I are fine just as we are and need no man to play with our hearts."

Kat gulped, hard. This woman was so brave. If only half of what she had heard was true, Alecia was a woman to be reckoned with. "Vard helped us on the road then left when we reached Brightcastle. He said he was on a mission, from the king?"

Alecia nodded. "He's a different man to the one I knew before." She knelt beside Hetty's cot and held the old woman's hand. "Dear Hetty, you must fight and get well."

"I've decided," Kat announced. "I'll take her to the castle, and Benae will have no choice but to help us. I've heard she is unable to resist the sick, so I'll force her to look upon Hetty's wasted countenance."

Alecia snorted yet again. It seemed Benae brought out the worst in her. "I wish you good luck, but I think the rumors you've heard greatly exaggerate Benae's compassion."

Kat ignored her. "We must decide how to get Hetty there without the journey killing her."

* * *

James rode Lightning, a silver stallion, through the gates of the castle and dismounted in the forecourt. The horse belonged to Cam and was one of a string of horses he owned, too numerous to ride. Lightning was James's favorite. A groom hurried up to help him dismount and led the horse away. James turned to survey the keep in all its glory.

The opal features on the face of the building sparkled in the sun, but he couldn't help a shudder at the knowledge the façade had been created centuries ago with the help of a witch. And recent events had also cast a pall over the structure. The sudden death of Prince Zialni was yet to be properly explained, in his opinion. Add to that the prior kidnapping of Princess Alecia and rumors of her mistreatment at the hands of her late father, and James had no real desire to set foot in the place.

However, he must if he wished to claim Princess Benae's patronage, along with gaining valuable intelligence. It was said Princess Alecia had recently returned with a young daughter, and, despite his reluctance, he was intrigued to discover more of the princess and her travels.

He gathered his thoughts and ascended the steps only to have the door open before he could knock. It seemed all footmen had a sixth sense when it came to the arrival of guests.

"Good morning, Master Tomel," said an aged footman. He gave a small bow. "The princess has been expecting you. Please follow me into the lower reception hall. Her Highness will join you presently."

No sooner had the words left the man's lips than the sound of a coach arriving drew their attention. James turned to find a public conveyance pulling up in the forecourt. A petitioner? The footman left James to approach the vehicle.

"You may not alight here, miss," the man said.

James didn't catch the reply, but the timbre of the voice pricked his ears. *Katrine?* He descended the steps and peered over the footman's shoulder.

"Can I help?"

"James, thank the Goddess." Katrine still wore breeches and a shirt, and dark shadows lurked beneath her eyes. Had she lost weight as well? "I need to see Princess Benae."

"This gentleman cannot help you, miss." The footman looked in at the frail Hetty. "Take this lady away before she spreads whatever she has to the palace."

Katrine gasped. "How dare you! This lady is worth ten of you, and I will not take her away until she is seen. I've heard the princess is a healer."

"She's nothing of the sort," the footman snapped. "Leave now, or I'll call the guards."

James cleared his throat. "Footman, I'm about to meet with the princess. Can't you have this carriage moved away from the stairs, and I'll speak to Princess Benae on the young lady's behalf?"

Katrine's grateful eyes looked ready to release a torrent of tears at his offer. "Thank you, James. You have no idea how sick Hetty is."

"I'll see what I can do. Footman?"

The old fellow frowned and shook his head, but ordered the driver to park the carriage near the gate. "Come with me, Master Tomel," he said as they walked, "but you're wasting your time, Sir. The princess won't endanger her child."

"Still, we shall ask her," James said, as he followed the footman into the small chamber.

He didn't have long to wait. A petite, dark-haired beauty in red velvet, accompanied by a teenaged maid, swept into the chamber fifteen minutes later. Princess Benae's dark brown hair was arranged in elaborate swirls and loops on the top of her head. But it was her eyes James noticed most. They were emerald green and full of intelligence.

He came forward and bowed as he took her offered hand. Her skin was rough as though she still did manual work. She was said to be an accomplished horsewoman, so perhaps that was the cause.

"Princess Benae," James said. "At last we meet. I can't wait to begin work on your circlet design."

She smiled. "I think I've chosen the correct jeweler if the pieces I've seen are anything to go by. They are exquisite."

A warm glow rose in his stomach. This woman knew her way around men. He had already decided he'd enjoy working with her. However, there was something he must tell her first.

"Before we start, Your Highness, there's another issue I must broach." He paused, uncertain how to begin. "There's a woman in the forecourt who has someone she wishes you to see. The old woman with her is gravely ill."

Benae took a step backward. "I can't help her. I won't risk my babe. He hasn't been strong since birth."

"Princess, it seems this woman will die, and you may be her last hope. I believe the young woman with her, Katrine, would've tried everything she could before troubling you."

Benae frowned. "I don't like to say no under those circumstances, but I can't risk my child."

"Do you think you could help, Princess?" James pressed. He saw the compassion in her eyes now, and knew she wanted to help against her better judgment. It was no easy choice to ask of her. Children often died in childhood, especially in the first year. And this child was the King's Heir.

She considered and then shook her head. "It's possible I could help, and I'm sorry for your young friend and for the ill woman, but I can't risk it, Master Tomel."

There was an indelicate snort at the door, and a tall, blonde woman with lilac eyes appeared. She wore the rich clothes of a lady. Or a princess. *Princess Alecia Zialni?*

Her lilac eyes speared James. "Excuse me, Sir, but I must interrupt." Her gaze snapped from James to the dark-haired princess. "*Stepmother,*" the blonde sneered. "You *will* help Hetty, or I'll see you regret it."

James winced. This was Princess Alecia alright.

"Hetty? The sick woman is the witch known as Hetty?" Benae's hands bunched into fists at her sides. "I'll *not* do as you say."

Alecia took a step toward her. "Keep your voice down. Some would kill Hetty on the strength of those words." She glared at James as though daring him to repeat what he had heard.

James raised his hands. "I have no interest in this Hetty you speak of."

"That is good, Sir," Alecia said. "Unlike my *stepmother,* I will defend my friends unto death."

James inclined his head. "I'm sure you are loyal, Princess."

Alecia narrowed her eyes. "Benae, you can't allow Hetty to die. She's important to me. I don't know what you hold against her – perhaps if you told me, I'd understand – but you can't stand by and allow her to die. Please help."

"I can't place my son at risk."

"I've been nursing her night and day and am as hale and hearty as the day I began," Alecia countered. "Iona is well too, and she isn't much older than your babe. Please. Don't let her die!"

Benae crossed to the window, her shoulders hunched, hands opening and closing at her sides. She clearly didn't wish to place her child at risk, but perhaps her conscience wouldn't allow her to walk away from Hetty either.

"I'll attend her, but she must remain outside." She turned to her maid. "Fetch my medicine box."

They walked out to the coach to find Katrine pacing up and down beside it. Benae stopped abruptly when she spotted the woman dressed in breeches and tunic.

Katrine approached and curtseyed. Breeches weren't made for that movement. James stifled a smile at the odd picture his beautiful friend presented.

"Princess Benae," she said, "thank you for attending my friend. I wouldn't trouble you but nothing I've done seems to pull Hetty from the grip of this disease."

Benae grimaced at the word. "Stand aside and I'll examine her. I have skill with herbs." Her maid arrived with a case and bowls. "You will all wait outside." Benae and her maid stepped inside the coach and closed the door.

Katrine joined James. "Thank you for convincing her to help."

"I did little. You should thank Princess Alecia. I think her words had most impact."

She wrung her hands. "I hope she's as skilled as they say." A frown crossed her brow, and she glanced at the carriage. "That's odd."

"What?"

"Never mind." She stood staring at the conveyance as if she could help by the sheer force of her will.

James touched her shoulder, and she turned to him. "How have you fared? You look tired."

She chewed her lip. "I've had little sleep since we arrived. Hetty was so ill I was scared if I left her side she might pass away. I don't know how she holds on, but she's strong."

"She's fortunate to have such a loyal friend," he said. "When I think of what you endured to be at her side…"

Katrine peered up at him. "I couldn't have done it without you. You've been …wonderful. Are your business dealings progressing as you would wish?"

Their conversation was so stilted it made James wish for the privacy to tell her how he felt – how she had changed him with her friendship and wild energy; how things once vital in his life no longer seemed important. But he couldn't do it here. Perhaps he shouldn't say anything.

"I suppose they are. That's if Princess Benae doesn't withdraw her patronage after this."

"I'm sorry," she said, a cloud dimming her gaze.

"My business with the princess can wait. I shouldn't have mentioned it. Please forgive me."

"Esta always implied I was selfish. Now I begin to understand what she meant. I must have my own way, I'm so focused on what I think is important, despite others having their own needs."

James tilted her chin, and her troubled eyes met his. "There's nothing selfish about you, Katrine. You're a true friend to Hetty and are brave and passionate. They're qualities you should treasure."

As hope lit Katrine's eyes, Princess Benae alighted from the carriage. Her head and shoulders were downturned, and she stumbled a little at the bottom of the coach stairs. She met Katrine's gaze. "I think your friend will recover. Good nursing is all she needs." She smiled at James. "I'm sorry, Master Tomel. May we meet tomorrow instead? I'm a little tired."

Princess Benae continued inside with her maid, but James didn't wish to lose the moment he and Katrine had just shared. He clutched her hand as she turned to climb back in the coach.

"Don't go," he said. "I need to see you."

Her eyes widened and then anger burned in them. "You had your chance and told me you needed to keep your distance. Now I must get Hetty back home. Perhaps you can call on me there." She opened the door of the coach then turned to him. "I'm sure you can discover where Hetty lives without any help from me."

And with those words he was dismissed. He was the older and wiser, but, with Katrine, he felt like a teenager on his first infatuation. She was so proud, too proud to beg for his company. But she was vulnerable too, with a sadness he'd dearly like to banish. The trouble was he had only added to her melancholy since he had known her.

He watched the coach move away, wondering when he might see her again. He turned to a footman. "Please tell the princess I'll visit her on the morrow at midmorning." It was then he saw Princess Alecia watching him. She approached.

She stood almost as tall as him and regarded him with interest. "You're James Tomel."

James swept a low bow. "It's a pleasure to meet you, Your Highness."

The princess inclined her head. "You met Vard Anton on your way here."

He nodded. "He was of assistance to us when we ran into trouble. I'm in his debt and would like to repay him. Can you tell me where he is?"

She shook her head. "I cannot. I simply wished to ask how he fared."

"He was well when last I saw him and that was entering Brightcastle some days ago. He implied he wished to see you."

Her eyebrows raised but it was her only response.

He exhaled. "He also said he had been pardoned for your abduction. Is that true? Vard Anton is now an operative of the king?"

Her lavender gaze turned grey. "It's true. But it was rescue, not abduction." Her eyes narrowed as she focused on him. "They say you're a spy master. Are you?"

He frowned. "You're blunt, Princess. If you needed to know that information, you wouldn't have to ask the question."

"And you, Master Tomel, are rude. I'm your princess, and, as such, you'll answer my question."

"I've already said as much as I intend." James bowed to her and turned to leave.

"Consider, Sir, there may come a day when you'll need my friendship, and that day may come sooner than you think."

James nodded and walked toward the stables to collect Lightning. When he passed back through the courtyard on his horse, there was no sign of Princess Alecia, but he had the feeling he had not seen the last of the feisty royal.

CHAPTER 12

A BELL rang downstairs, and Kat groaned. She rolled over in bed and pushed herself up, dragging the blanket around her shoulders.

"A moment!" She was glad Hetty was recovered enough to ring the bell, but did she have to ring it so often? It seemed like Kat had just touched her head to the pillow, and, indeed, it was still dark outside. She descended the stairs and entered the kitchen where Hetty sat in her cot adjacent to the fire.

"There you are, girl!" Hetty said. "I was about to get it myself."

Kat ground her teeth on a snarky reply. "What do you want, Hetty? And what time is it?"

"Time you were up, young Kat," she said. "It's past five, and I'd like my breakfast. Stoke the fire, will you?"

Kat rattled around in the kitchen, adding wood to the fire and placing the kettle and pot on the hooks. "How about a nice cup of tea while the porridge cooks?"

"Thank you. Don't forget the bread."

As if Kat ever could with Hetty to remind her. It was two days since they had seen Princess Benae, and the change in the old woman was miraculous. She had put on weight, and her breathing was almost normal. Even the cough was nearly gone.

Kat paused as she pondered the astounding changes in her old friend. Benae must have magic at her disposal. It would explain the

112

sensation Kat had experienced when Benae had been in the coach with Hetty - the prickling of magic. There was no other explanation.

The thought made her despondent. Kat was one of the strongest witches Hetty had ever seen, yet she was unable to cure her sick friend. She had thrown every spell and potion she could think of into Hetty's care, and all she had succeeded in doing was to prevent her slipping over the brink. It wasn't good enough! *She* was not good enough.

"What is it, girl?" Hetty's voice slipped through the fog clogging her mind.

Kat fiddled with the pot and tea leaves. "Nothing. I'm glad you're feeling better." She turned away. "I'll get the bread going."

"Katrine Aranati, you will stop your fussing and tell me what's wrong."

Kat sighed and pulled a chair up to Hetty's bed. She met the older woman's concerned expression.

"I'm afraid you were wrong about my powers," she said. "I couldn't help you when you were ill." The admission made her failure more real. Not so long ago, Kat thought magic might be her savior - that it would pull her from melancholy and give her purpose. Now she didn't know what to believe.

"I wondered when you would fall into this hole," Hetty said.

"What do you mean? You've been waiting for me to fail?" Kat's temper simmered just short of the boil. Hetty was so devious when she wished to be. Centuries of living had taught the old woman all there was to know about people, and she used it to her advantage.

"Don't get all in a flap!" Hetty said, warm air from the fire making her spiky grey hair dance. "I meant the life of a witch is full of challenges, especially when we are young. There is so much to learn, and it's easy to think we know it all when we're at the start of our journey."

"You said I could be the most powerful of our kind!"

"And so you might be. However, it depends on you and which paths you take. It also doesn't mean you won't fail from time to time. And each one of us has inherent talents. Do you believe healing is your strongest?"

Kat huffed. "Not if the last week is anything to go by. I could do little while ..." She hadn't decided whether to tell Hetty who had saved her. Perhaps she should keep Benae's secrets.

"Princess Benae's aid delivered a magical turnaround in my health," Hetty said, plucking at the coverlet.

"You know!"

"Of course I do, dear. I wasn't so sick I wasn't aware of what was happening around me. I saw what you did for me, and I knew when you took me to the castle. Despite fearing me, Princess Benae did her very best. I felt her magic surge through me and believed I would be well. It's quite a gift she has, but it's only healing magic and none other."

"Why does she fear you?"

"She thinks I had something to do with the death of her first husband."

"And did you?"

Kat didn't wish to believe Hetty capable of harming anyone, but was she being naïve? After all, disguised as Lady Star, Kat had been responsible for deaths during her battles at sea. Her escapades had never come to light in the recent trial against her brother-in-law. But those days were over.

"It's possible I may have contributed to his demise, although I had no intention to do more than make him impotent. I wasn't aware at the time that the prince already had trouble in the bedroom and was taking all manner of herbs to aid his performance."

Kat covered her ears. "Enough! I have no wish to hear the details. I'm glad you weren't to blame."

"Don't be dim, girl. Our magic can be used as a weapon. Any time we wield it, we have to be ready to accept the consequences."

I am, I believe. It was something that bore examination when she had more time.

"Don't think you've distracted me from the real purpose of this talk, and that is to scrutinize your magic and your current wretchedness."

"I'm fine, Hetty. You're getting well, and that's the most important thing."

"And I thank you from the bottom of my heart for all you did. You kept me from death, and, when you couldn't do more, you sought the help of the only person who could. Did anyone else think of that?"

"There was only Alecia, and she was as worried as I." Kat shuddered at how close they had come to losing Hetty.

"Alecia relied upon you to help, but when you couldn't you didn't give up," Hetty said. "Part of being a sorceress is knowing your limits. You recognized you couldn't do any more, and I thank you for taking me to Benae."

Kat stared at her friend. How could she see this as anything other than a failure? "It's kind of you to say so."

Hetty snorted. "You're stubborn, child! Every witch and wizard has a range of powers, and some are greater than others. Some are healers, others are warriors, still others have the power to alter nature and the elements. The list is long. You have been a warrior all your adult life, so I'm not surprised healing isn't your strong magic."

Kat's mouth fell open. It made sense. She had so much to learn!

"Now you must decide if it means enough for you to turn your back on love and pursue the lonely life of a sorceress." Hetty's dark eyes bored into Kat, challenging her as she always did. How had she thought she could hide anything from the old woman?

"I don't have a love in my life."

"What of the dark-haired master? Alecia sensed a connection between you. That's why I need to say this. You can't devote your life to magic if you have a man. It's one or the other. Why do you think I never married?"

Kat looked down at her hands. Hands which could nurture and love - or destroy. Could she turn her back on all that potential for the sake of love? And what of James? Did he feel that way about her? She looked at Hetty. "It's a decision for another day."

"You don't deny it then?"

Kat's mouth dropped open. "You were fishing! You didn't know for sure about James."

Hetty nodded, her eyes gleaming. "I suspected. You were different, pre-occupied. I can usually read the signs. James Tomel is known to me. His work is exquisite. How did you meet him?"

It seemed she had known James forever, but Kat was startled to realize it was less than two weeks since she nearly ran him down. So much had transpired since then. While Hetty knew of the night hounds and the tragedy of the dead newborn, Kat had been vague about the identity of the man involved. She told Hetty the full story including her trip to Brightcastle, leaving out certain embarrassing incidents. "What of the night hounds, Hetty? How do I banish them?"

"If they're drawn to your magic, that makes you special. I've not heard of them in over fifty years, but I've heard of witches who were dogged by the beasts. If you're one of them, it may mean you can't turn your back on the life of a sorceress."

Kat kneeled in front of the old woman's pallet. "What do you mean?"

Hetty's eyes darted around the kitchen before finally landing on Kat. "Would you like to raise a family with those beasts around?"

Kat laughed. "You imply I won't be able to shake them."

"I'm implying nothing of the sort." Hetty huffed. "I'm *telling* you, they could be here to stay. Better get used to dodging them, or find a way to live with the things."

Kat sat back on her heels, heart thudding, and the blood roaring in her ears. How naïve had she been to think reaching Brightcastle could protect her from the danger of the night hounds?

* * *

Four days after seeing Katrine at the castle, James was still no closer to visiting her. He had set out several times, but on each occasion, something held him back. Some force made him question if he should have any more to do with the enticing lady and her wild magic. It was foolish of him to contemplate a life with her. She had never been in his plans and was totally unsuitable. She would only bring chaos into his world.

He was so confused about the whole issue, he decided to take a ride to clear his head. He collected Lightning from the stable and headed for the meadow. James had often ridden there when in the city. It lay to the north, and the ride was pleasant. In summer, the roads were edged in all manner of wildflowers, and the meadow itself was a favored site for picnics and archery practice - preferably not at the same time.

However, in winter, the wonders were not so numerous. A light fall of snow covered his tracks as he made them but at least there was no breeze to make the trip colder. Besides, Lightning needed the exercise, cooped up as he was in a stable most of the time.

As James rode, he weighed up the two women in his life, though Katrine could hardly be called his woman. Melanis expected him to make their betrothal formal any day now, yet he couldn't make himself visit *her* either. She offered so much. Before Katrine, he had yearned for the stability Melanis offered. Their worlds could merge without as much as a breath of disturbance. Once he had yearned for such predictability, but now something deep within shied away from it like a horse confronted by a snake.

And Katrine! She was anything but predictable. She was wild and spontaneous, and he was drawn to her more than he had ever experienced with anyone. They struck sparks together, and nothing would ever be boring. And the physical connection they shared eclipsed his relationship with Melanis. He couldn't get the fiery sorceress out of his thoughts or his dreams.

He needed to speak with her and judge if there could ever be anything permanent between them. Just contemplating her as a mate left him confounded!

Mind swirling with uncertainty, James arrived at the meadow just as a sizzling noise attracted his attention. A fireball the size of his chest smashed into a tree ten paces to his right, and Lightning reared.

James tightened his hold on the reins and spun the horse in a tight circle once his four hoofs were back on solid ground, patting him on the side of the neck. The beast trembled, his eyes rolling wildly, but James stayed in the saddle in case Lightning should try to bolt.

Katrine skidded to a halt in front of the horse, almost sending the beast into another panic. "James! I didn't see you! Are you harmed?"

He dismounted, and she grasped his elbows, her starry eyes awhirl. He warmed under the heat of her examination. "I'm well. No thanks to you and your…magic."

"Thank the Goddess! I inverted the spell so the hounds wouldn't be drawn, but it interferes with my control." She chewed her lip. "I must make it work."

Her dark hair lay in wild waves over her shoulders, her breasts pressed against the fabric of her tunic and she was still wearing those skintight breeches that left too little to the imagination. He tried to look away with little success. "No harm done, but do you think you should be causing an exhibition where anyone might see and hear?"

She sighed. "I needed to get out. I've been cooped up with Hetty for days. And I had some thinking to do. I find being out in nature helps."

"Thinking?"

She turned and walked away from him toward the closest archery target. Drawing a knife from her boot, Katrine flung it at the target, hitting dead center. She pulled another knife from her other boot and one from her sleeve. The results were the same - three knives all in the bull's eye.

"Impressive," James said. He tied Lightning to a branch and joined her.

"Is it? Perhaps it doesn't mean anything that I can throw a knife and cast a fireball. Perhaps I'm on the wrong path."

James approached. "Why doubt yourself now?"

She turned to him, and he ached at the raw pain in her eyes. "I'm a freak. If I embrace my talents, I'll have to turn my back on everything other women hold dear - husband, family, friends."

James grabbed her hands. "Katrine, you're not a freak. You're beautiful, and passionate, and so talented. I can't stand to hear you call yourself names."

Kat glanced at their hands. "*You* turned your back on me after... after..."

"It wasn't a rejection of *you*."

"What else could it be?" Her gaze searched his. "That night changed my life."

He brushed his knuckles down the softness of her cheek, and her eyes fluttered closed. "I've not been able to forget how you looked," he whispered.

The hope that flared in her brilliant orbs nearly undid him. He had the power to lift her up or crush her. Which would it be? He couldn't begin to guess, and he lowered his lips to hers, drawn by the passion swirling between them. What started as a gentle exploration was met with fire and desperation from Katrine. Before James could blink, she slammed her body against his, her hands threaded up into his hair. Each touch of her nails on his scalp threatened to send him crazy.

He pulled back, uncertain of what he wanted, of what she needed. Their eyes met, and, in them, he had his answer. At least he saw she wanted him with a desperation he had never imagined. Need swirled in his gut, driving his lips back to hers. He relished every inch of her body as it molded itself to him, her leg sweeping up to wrap around his buttocks as though to open herself to him.

"Finish what we began the other night, James," she breathed.

Those words were all he needed. This wasn't about clear thinking; it was about need, and lust, and deep driving hunger he was no longer capable of fighting. He searched for a suitable space and found a small clearing in the trees with a log at one end. James led Katrine over to the snowy space and laid his cloak on the ground, then pulled her down beside him.

He opened her cloak, his eyes fixed to hers so he would see any doubt she possessed. He saw only passion and desperation in her fiery expression. His fingers fumbled on her tunic buttons as he anticipated their union, but she brushed his hands aside, and soon her tunic and shirt hung open. James bent to lick her nipples, first one then the other, sucking as hard as he dared. She groaned, and the sound went straight to his groin. He was so hard it was painful.

"Take me, James. Now. I don't want to wait." She pushed him back against his cloak and undid his breeches, pushing his shirt and undershirt high and leaning down to kiss his abdomen, all the way up to his nipples.

Katrine stood and removed her boots and breeches, revealing long shapely legs. She allowed him to look, and he couldn't believe he was fortunate enough to have this goddess ready to give him her most precious possession. He knelt and grasped her thighs then licked her slick folds, his tongue piercing where no man had ever been. He buried his face in her, his tongue slicing in and out of her as she trembled and quaked. She screamed with the fury of her climax.

Instead of coming down slowly, Katrine seized his shoulders and pushed him backward, freeing him from his loosened breeches and straddling him. She impaled herself on his rod with one quick movement, her eyes widening as it speared her core. She uttered another primal scream and started to move, her fingernails scoring his chest.

James was gone in an instant, her savagery sweeping aside his pledge to take her gently. It was too late for tenderness. Katrine had pushed him over the edge, but damned if she would dominate him as she wanted to. He gripped her buttocks and sat up, flipping her underneath him and thrusting back into her. She took all of him, her head lolling back, moans rocking her body. Her fingers seized the folds of the cloak beneath her, and she screamed his name as she thrust against him. James had her breasts in his hands, pinching the nipples as he thrust once, twice, and sent himself over the edge into oblivion while she stiffened beneath him.

He came back down from a place he had never been. Glory and savagery had met in one blinding episode of lust and love that shouldn't have existed. James glanced down and saw wonder in her eyes. In that moment, he realized he'd never forget her. Katrine Aranati was extraordinary, and he wanted her with every beat of his heart. He kissed her gently, reverently, but she responded with fire, clutching his head and thrusting her tongue into his mouth.

Before he could think, they were moving again in the dance older than time. It was sinful to want more of what they had shared, but he did. He knew that beyond any doubt. His desire mounted, matched by hers, and soon their scorching heat consumed them. The clearing rang with the screams of their union - fierce, hot, and indescribable.

* * *

Kat floated back to the reality of a cold clearing in the forest, James still sheathed within her. Despite the chill, their union felt right, a completion, as though her whole life had been building to this moment. She looked into his eyes and watched as contented desire turned to horror.

"Don't you dare regret what we did," she said as he pulled away from her. She drew her tunic and shirt over her naked breasts, gulping down the fear that so quickly replaced ecstasy.

"What have we done?" He stood and pulled on his discarded shirt then re-laced his breeches. He helped her up and shook the snow off his cloak before throwing it around his shoulders. "This was never meant to happen," he said, gesturing between the two of them. "And now you might be with child, your life changed forever by one careless coupling."

She held up her hand. "Two! And stop it right now. I'll take the herb mix to prevent conception if it's what you want; only please…no regrets. It was the most wonderful moment of my life."

His eyes softened, and he stepped closer to sweep his fingertips over her cheeks. "You must forget this and move past it. You and I were never destined to be together. Take the potion just in case, and leave this in the past where it belongs."

Kat couldn't believe she was hearing those words after the passion they had shared. "How can you turn your back on us? Was this merely lust for you?"

"There is no 'us'. I told you that once before." He didn't meet her eyes but completed dressing and fetched his horse. "Now dress so we can return to the city, before someone comes along."

She stared at him, willing him to look at her, so she might determine if he spoke the truth. She wasn't imagining the depth of their connection - she wasn't. He kept walking away, and Kat had no choice but to pull on her breeches and tidy herself up. She retrieved her cloak and strode to her horse, stowing her knives in their holders as she went.

When she pulled herself up on Demon, James was already on the road back to the city.

CHAPTER 13

JAMES saw Katrine home and turned his horse in the direction of Lady Stenmore's manor house. It was past time he gave her an answer, and now he knew what it would be. His body still hummed with the passion he had found in Katrine's arms, a moment in his life he'd never forget. But he couldn't allow her to hope for a life with him. He was all but engaged.

While he and Melanis were perfectly suited, Kat wasn't what he needed in a life partner. Equally, James couldn't foresee a world in which a spymaster could join with a witch. She didn't need him in her life like a millstone around her neck. She needed to be free to be herself, a sorceress of rare talent, even if it must be in secret.

He shook his head, trying to dispel the fever that fired his blood. Katrine Aranati wouldn't be easy to leave behind, and he already accepted he'd never forget her. However, it was time to move forward, to give Melanis her answer, and get on with making the future. The thought gave James comfort as he negotiated the frosty streets. By the time he arrived at the Stenmore mansion, he was calmer than he had been in a long time. Perhaps it was proof his decision was the correct one?

He was shown into the parlor by Roth, only, this time, Melanis was already present, seated in her favorite chair before the fire. He crossed the room and took her hand, bringing it to his lips for a fleeting kiss.

Her jaw tightened at his gesture. "You do keep a lady waiting, James."

"Yes," he said, his gaze sweeping over her. She looked tired, as though the wait had aged her. "I'm sorry, but I needed the time to get my head settled."

"I hear you met your dark-haired traveling companion at the palace. I also hear she is stunning." Melanis squared her shoulders. "Have you come to tell me it's over between us?"

James had thought he was ready for this moment, but the memory of Katrine, as she screamed in completion below him, made him hesitate. Melanis pounced.

"I don't care if you throw us on the scrap heap." She looked away, into the fire. "I'll find another. Perhaps not in time to have children, but, nevertheless, I'll have a worthwhile existence."

James watched as she tried to come to terms with a life without him. He remembered all the times they had shared, the love they had made, the plans, the joy in each other.

"I want to make our engagement official, Melanis."

* * *

Kat let herself into Hetty's home, still lost in a world where James told her he would love her forever. It would happen. She could make it true. She squared her shoulders and steeled herself to face Hetty.

As she entered the kitchen, Hetty turned from the hearth and froze.

"Whatever is the matter, child?" She placed the pot on the table and hurried to take Kat's hands. "You're frozen, and you look as though you've been rolling in the forest."

Damn the woman! She was always so observant. "Don't be silly, Hetty. Demon and I enjoyed a gallop back from the meadow. We may have hit a few branches on the way."

"Something happened, and you'll tell me what!" Her eyes scooted all over Kat. "Someone has taken advantage of you. Tell me who!"

She shook her head. "I tell you it's nothing like that."

"I have eyes in my head and can see the signs. You went out a girl and returned a woman."

Kat huffed out a breath. "You're so dramatic, Hetty. I'm well, and you're imagining things. Now drop this, or I'll …" To Kat's horror, tears filled her eyes and spilled down her cheeks. Damn it! She couldn't even control her own body!

Hetty drew her to a chair by the fire and made her sit, then pushed a cup of tea into her hands. "Drink, Kat, and then you'll tell me everything."

She closed her eyes, desperate for composure. She drew in long gulps of the honeyed tea, enjoying the warmth that spiraled down her body. Eventually, she was ready to speak.

"The man I traveled here with arrived at the meadow when I was practicing with my fireballs. And, before you start lecturing, I inverted the spells. No hounds were drawn to me." She closed her eyes, reliving the life-changing moment when she welcomed James into her body. How could she explain to Hetty the exhilaration she had experienced at his hands? Or the desperation when he rejected her?

When she opened her eyes, Hetty's stare trapped her, compelling her to speak.

"We talked. It's complicated. There's something holding him back from me, and I'm not sure what it is. We kissed, and, before either of us realized it, we had coupled. It was the most wonderful experience of my life." No need to tell Hetty she had attacked James like an animal. Her face heated at the thought.

Hetty hissed. "You may be with child. I must mix the medicine."

Kat held up her hand. "There will be time later. That's not what has me upset."

"It's not? You said it was wonderful. What else happened?"

She sighed. "He wants nothing more to do with me." Her tears spilled again as Hetty paced back and forth across the kitchen.

"I'll soon find this man and teach him not to fool with young ladies," her friend said. "I suppose now you've given him what he sought he has cast you off?"

Kat stood. "It's not like that at all. He loves me, I'm sure he does."

"Funny way of showing it," Hetty muttered.

"I just have to get past his reservations."

"Which are what? How dare he take your virginity and then disrespect you? I'm not without power in this town. Princess Alecia could make his life difficult indeed."

Kat threw her hands up. "Stop! I must resolve this on my own. Promise me you won't interfere."

She knew the stubborn look on her friend's face meant trouble. "I mean it, Hetty. You must let me work this out. I know I can convince him to take a chance with me."

Hetty screwed up her face, her whiskery chin quivering. "If you have to convince him, how much of a catch can he be, girl?"

"He's handsome, and smart, and so talented. He's a gentleman and terribly loyal to his friends. James is all I ever dreamed of in a husband, but he holds the belief that our worlds can never meld. My magic unnerves him, and I think he had a very different life mapped out than the one he would have with me."

"It's a lot of man you have there, young Kat." Hetty said, sitting opposite and fixing her with a sympathetic eye. "Are you sure what you feel for him is real? Have you considered what I said about the life of a sorceress? It seems to me this man of yours may have a point. And if so, he had no right taking your maidenhead."

Kat grabbed both of Hetty's hands in her own. "Stop saying that! It doesn't matter. I gave it to him freely and would do so again in a heartbeat. You place too much importance on my being a virgin. If you expect me to live the life of a sorceress, what does it matter?"

Hetty crossed her arms under her breasts. "It's the principle of the thing. It's not right, and he should be held accountable for his actions."

"You will *not* be the one to do that." She fixed her friend with the unblinking stare which usually had people looking away, but she should've known better than to think Hetty would be daunted. Not that she really imagined she could intimidate her. She only wished to impress upon her that she could handle her own affairs.

Hetty stood and drew Kat up with her, clutching her elbows with boney hands. "I love you like a daughter, Katrine Aranati. This moment is a crossroads for you, and you must make the correct turning. If you take the counsel of your heart, it may be a mistake. Please promise you'll make no rash decisions."

Kat drew Hetty close, more tears spilling down her cheeks. "And you're like a mother to me. I value your advice, and I'll try to keep it in mind as I deal with James." It was an easy promise to make, but harder to keep in light of the desire that had raged through her in the meadow.

She was more certain now she could convince James to take a chance on her, whatever her promise to Hetty. She could have a life of magic *and* a loving man, and she would if it was the last thing she did.

Fiery determination blazed through her, and Kat realized her melancholy had subsided. Had it been seared from her in the heat of passion? And, if that was the case, wasn't it proof that loving James was the right course?

Now all she had to do was convince *him*.

* * *

James greeted Cal and his wife, Sorrel, at the front door of Stenmore Manor and was engulfed in a hug by his friend.

"Congratulations, James," Cal said as Sorrel disappeared in search of Melanis. "No more doubts then?"

He escorted Cal into the small parlor and closed the door. "I never had doubts about Melanis," he said, handing his friend a goblet of mulled wine. "I had to come to a decision about the direction I wished my life to take."

"You look more relaxed than I've seen you in a long time. When is the wedding?"

"Mel wants it soon. We've waited long enough - I can't believe she doesn't hold it against me."

"She loves you."

James shook his head. "This isn't a love match. It's a meeting of minds and lives, a marriage of convenience. This way, there's no drama or upheaval."

Cal frowned. "I think you may be underestimating Melanis. She has real feelings for you."

Fear uncurled in his gut. If Melanis loved him…he didn't know how to relate to her under those circumstances. His mind flew to the instant connection he had with Katrine. Right from literally running into her, they struck sparks off each other. It was how he had finally concluded they could never be together. He couldn't control her or his desire for her, and it terrified him.

"You appear disturbed by my observation," Cal said. "I thought you'd be filled with joy to have won over the most eligible widow in the region."

James ran his fingers through his hair. What he really wanted to do was run far away from Brightcastle and the trap he had set for himself.

"Love was never part of the plan. I don't love Melanis, and I never will." James paced back and forth across the parlor, his mind frantically seeking a way out of the mess he had gotten himself into. If Melanis loved him, he could never be sure their relationship wouldn't evolve into an ugly distortion of the civilized pattern it currently followed.

Cal stepped in front of him. "If I had guessed how this would upset you, I wouldn't have mentioned it. Forget I said anything. I may be wrong anyway."

James held his hand up. "No, you're right. I should have seen it myself. It's why she waited for me to fumble my way to commitment."

"Does it change anything? When all is said and done, a loving wife is a precious gift."

James pulled himself together. "Of course, it is." No need to let his friend see his distress. He didn't understand James's need for order and control. Both these things he thought he had with Melanis. Now, he wasn't sure. How long would it be before she realized he wasn't enough and made his life a living hell? How long before she made demands he couldn't accept?

"Let's join the ladies for dinner," he said and led the way, his body in Stenmore House and his frantic mind hunting far and wide for a solution.

* * *

Kat set out early the next morning in search of James. She had no idea where he lived, but how difficult could it be to track him down? All she need do was ask in the market. Someone would know him.

A frigid wind blew from the north, and Kat drew her coat tight about her body. She wore her usual garb, and the looks of the townsfolk turned curiously in her direction. Once in the market, she inquired and was given directions to the shop of the master goldsmith. Kat smirked. She should have guessed James would seek the company of his own kind. Apparently, the shop and residence were located near the castle.

She kept her eyes downcast as she walked, only raising them to avoid walking into other brave souls who were out this early in the morning. On the way, she spied the cathedral and entered the forecourt, pausing to admire a statue of the Goddess.

She continued through an arch and into the chamber of worship, eager to spend a few moments before the brazier that always burned there. Perhaps she could light a candle for her family and one for Hetty.

She took a candle from the shelves that fanned out either side of the fire and lit it, placing it on the circular stone platform beside the brazier. She lit another for Hetty then said a prayer to the Goddess. She was the only one in the building and a deep peace descended upon her.

She closed her eyes and drew in the serenity, wrapping it around herself like a cloak against the trouble of the outside world.

All would be well. She would convince James they should be together, and she could have her vocation as well. Perhaps the kingdom of Thorius might one day accept witchcraft for all the good it could do.

Feeling better than she had in weeks, she turned to leave the cathedral, but stopped idly to read the marriage banns posted in the vestibule.

Her blood ran cold as she read the single note fluttering in the blustery wind. Her heart slowed as though time itself stood still.

It is with great joy that
Lady Melanis Stenmore of Brightcastle and
James Tomel, Master Jeweler of Costa,
announce their intention to wed.
Any person who can name a reason this couple cannot be united
should present themselves at the next service
and state their objection.
Praise the Goddess
Aphra Havisa, High Priestess

Kat pulled the notice from the wall and screwed it up, channeling a burst of magic into the paper ball so it turned instantly to ash. The dust fell from her fingers, but the destruction did nothing to lift her anger. How could she get this involved with James and not know the man had a fiancée? A fiancée. *A fiancée*!

With each repetition, her fury grew and, with her fury, her magic. Kat fed the beast within as over and over in her mind tumbled images of her encounters with James during the past weeks. Encounters which had meant something - everything - to her. But it seemed he had led her on, only to cast her aside when she gave him what he sought. He had played her like a harp, made her purr under his hands like a faithful cat.

Well, this feline had claws, and she would not be any man's plaything.

She tuned back to the brazier and lit every candle with one sweep of her hand. Leaving the cathedral ablaze with candlelight, she strode out into the street. Heat rose within, stronger than ever before. She was a swirling figure of magic, no longer Katrine Aranati but a mystic vessel, capable of anything.

No longer would she wait on any man's pleasure, and she wouldn't allow him to dump her back into the abyss she had dwelt in. She had power - more than she had ever realized - and she would use it, not be afraid; not hide like a worm under a rock.

She walked through the town square, the blast of her magic lighting each candle, hearth and torch within one hundred paces. She sensed the flare of kitchen hearths and candles, empty fireplaces and dozens of torches that had been extinguished with the daylight.

The ground trembled with her footsteps, and she focused inwards, calming the response of the earth. She couldn't give herself away so clearly as to have an earthquake follow her through the city. Birds launched themselves from eaves and rooftops and flew squawking into the sky. Cats stared at her from the depths of alleys as she passed, and dogs ran howling. All except for that dog...and that one.

Kat stopped in the middle of the street, almost at her destination. The night hounds had found her. She looked into their red eyes and knew no fear. They were *hers*. Instinctively, she knew, though she didn't understand why. She snapped her fingers and four of the beasts fell in behind her. She continued and soon found the goldsmith's house.

"*James*." She spoke in her mind.

He appeared at an upper window. Seconds later, he stepped through the front door into the street.

"Katrine..." His tone was low, guarded. Dark shadows lay below his eyes and his hair rested upon his shoulders. "What are you doing here? With them?"

She placed her hands on her hips and held her head high. He would never suspect how his betrayal had wounded her. "They're mine now. They're true to me. Unlike you."

He raised his hand to stop her, but she gave an abrupt shake of her head.

"I loved you, James. I gave my whole self to you, only yesterday, and today I discover you're betrothed. How long?"

He took a deep breath. Let him lie. She would know it.

"Two years we've been friends," he said.

"And how long lovers?"

"Half of that time."

"Have you told her about me?" Her voice was cold, though she boiled inside.

"No."

"So… I suppose I wasn't around long enough for it to matter."

"Can I speak now?" He stepped closer.

One of the hounds growled, but James reached out and grasped her hands. Hands that tingled with magic.

"I'll never forget you, Katrine, if it's any consolation."

"As if it could ever be enough," she spat. "Do you recall our union yesterday?" Was it only yesterday he had set her world trembling with the power of his love making? "You made me a woman, and today you branded me with your treachery. Two lovers…will you tell her what you've done?"

"She suspected there was another woman but, now we're officially betrothed, Melanis won't care."

She closed her eyes and clutched his fingers one last time - a moment she would have to survive on for the rest of her life. When she opened her eyes, the man she loved stood before her, and, for a brief moment, he showed her what was within his heart. What she saw wasn't treachery or betrayal. It was pure love, and it was for her.

She stepped back. "You've made your decision. If I had realized I would've fought harder. I don't begin to understand you, James, but I'll respect your choice. Be happy."

Kat turned and walked away without a backward glance, her hounds trotting at her heels. She had to dispel the power gathered within, so she led the hounds deep into the woods, blasting her magic at sick, scrawny trees as she went, turning them to ash, until weariness dragged at each step. Then she turned and walked back into town, leaving the hounds in the forest.

Back at Hetty's, she shed her wet clothes and boots, and bathed herself before the fire in the kitchen. Hetty said not a word, but fetched clean clothes, dark eyes considering her all the while. Then Kat climbed the stairs to her bed and fell into a deep sleep.

CHAPTER 14

KAT leaned against the nursery doorframe and watched her sister and baby nephew. Mica grew quickly, and Esta looked serene and blissful as she suckled the babe. Perhaps this was what life was about. Maybe Hetty was wrong. Kat had been back on the Aranati estate for four months, having left Brightcastle soon after her confrontation with James. With Hetty fully recovered, there was nothing to keep her in the city, and she wouldn't place herself at risk of seeing James and his happy bride.

Life had settled into the normal routine with some exceptions. She helped more on the estate, using her powers to fell trees and chop firewood or boil water for bathing. She practiced at herb lore, and felt she might even save lives one day. She was also studying alchemy. She believed she was close to turning lead into gold and had already made silver from bronze. Oh, how James would ache to have her in his life now!

But no, he had chosen another, and, if she was being honest with herself, her abilities with metals would change nothing. There was something blocking his belief in their love. She had witnessed his deep feelings the last time she saw him and failed to understand how he could walk away. Why had he chosen the Stenmore woman? Every time she asked the question, she came up with one answer. James just couldn't accept Kat's natural essence - her sorcery. He'd said as much before, after she confessed her gift.

His rejection of her burned. It seemed unfair that he should spurn her on the strength of something she had no control over. But after several weeks of wallowing in her disappointment, she locked the hurt away where it couldn't harm her. Although she couldn't have James, Kat hadn't given up on love, just set it aside for another day and time. A man would come along and cherish her for what she was, not merely see her as a beautiful and exciting dalliance.

Meanwhile, Kat decided she wouldn't waste a moment more pining over James. She refused to discuss him with Esta, and, each time his face popped into her head, she thrust it away. She kept herself in a fevered state, her days filled with work and study and movement toward a future all of them were excited about. And, once a month when the moon was full, she saddled Demon and rode into the forest to connect with her hounds.

By some means, they realized when she would come and were always waiting at the clearing she had designated. Kat placed flat rocks for each of them to sit on - twenty-one at the present time. She didn't know if there might be more in future, but it mattered not. Her greeting involved laying her right palm on each dog's head. She called him or her by the name she had decreed, and the beast would lick her wrist in answer. They seemed to have forgiven her for the deaths of their friends, but she still experienced an aching sadness when she remembered the hounds who had been killed.

After the greeting, she would mount Demon and join the hunt. Her horse was used to the dogs by now, but still stamped a hoof and snorted if any dared approach. If he could breathe fire, he would. The same couldn't be said for her. She was still in disbelief that the hounds didn't wish to hurt her. They saw her as a leader, but she faked her bravery around them. She schooled the tremor from her voice and had trained her heart and lungs to the slow rhythm of the truly courageous.

Nonetheless, it was becoming easier to accept her authority over the beasts. Perhaps one day the mantle might settle fully on her shoulders, and she'd understand what it meant. The night hounds hadn't been seen for half a century, and Kat wondered if they'd been waiting for a new leader. Or did they come in response to a need the kingdom had?

She allowed her instinct to guide her, leading her out into the forest at full moon, naming the beasts, the greeting, the hunt...She was one with them, and they with her. They'd be a formidable fighting force if ever they were needed, but Kat kept them secret from her family. When they hunted, she took her knives and bow, on occasion killing a rabbit or a deer herself for the hounds. It was a welcome supplement to the prey they caught, and joy filled her heart when she watched them eating food she had provided.

Sometimes, Kat dreamed of the hunt - was one of the hounds, her hard pads pounding over dirt and grass, her fangs slicing into fresh, warm meat. She awoke from those dreams in a state of euphoria, but they also disturbed her. With each dream, she understood the hounds more. Was it their way of teaching her what she needed to learn? Or was she becoming one of them? Was it the product of her overactive imagination?

Whatever her life had become, she was fulfilled, almost happy, and the black melancholy she once suffered was no longer the dominant force in her life. She was very glad of that.

* * *

James broke away from his daydream for the tenth time in the last hour. He was getting nothing done in his workshop, and Princess Benae wanted her tiara completed before the end of the month. It had already taken far longer than it ever should have. At this rate, there'd be no referrals from the royal.

He sighed and pushed away the beautiful piece with its golden scrolls and emeralds. Perhaps a walk might help. He could call in on his network and collect the latest news from the pigeons. He threw a light cloak about his shoulders and pulled the hood over his head to protect his anonymity. Thus prepared, he stepped from his shop and started up the main street, trying to keep his attention on the businesses he passed. Nothing seemed to hold his interest these days, not since his return from Brightcastle three months ago, and he wondered if he'd ever be welcome in that city again.

He had broken his engagement to Melanis.

It wasn't fair to commit to a life with her when Katrine dominated his thoughts. She haunted his dreams, sometimes taking the form of a night hound. The sparkling blue eyes always gave her away within the beast. During his waking hours, her image was more difficult to banish.

It must stop, but how could he make his traitorous heart forget the woman he loved? *Loved?* He hadn't thought himself susceptible to the condition, but what else was it? He relived their love-making time and again, his body an aching mess of desire nothing could cure.

James entered a tavern and took a seat. He ordered an ale and a meal and rested his head against the wall near the cold fireplace. Perhaps he could drink himself into oblivion? That was unlike him, too. He drank more and more of late. At first, it was to make himself forget he couldn't perform with Melanis. Now it was the cursed dreams that turned him to the bottle. If he wasn't careful, he'd drink himself to death or at least into the poor house. Where was the carefully established and hard-won control that had always governed his adult life?

It had gone, that was the truth! Ever since Katrine Aranati careened headlong into his life, he had been blown like a feather on the wind, and with no more direction. At times he almost succumbed to the panic that seized him, but he would breathe his way through the fear, focused on the steady life force that surged within. He tried not to think of Katrine at times like that, but more often than not it was her dancing eyes and saucy smile which banished the last of his panic.

He sighed heavily and took a long drink from his tankard. This had to end.

CHAPTER 15

KAT bounced her nephew on her knee, and he giggled. Mica was the light of her life, and sometimes the ache to have a child of her own was almost physical. On occasion she could almost believe he was hers, with his dark hair and blue eyes. But she might never have a child of her own and she had best get used to that possibility.

Nothing had changed within Kat's world. The seasons rolled by as ever they had, and life on the farm grew prosperous as the end of summer approached. The time of the full moon approached, and she looked forward to it, but she couldn't dispel the nagging fear that struck whenever she thought of her hounds. Her dreams were more vivid than ever over the past two weeks. The hounds she met in them yapped at her, though they rarely did so in the waking world. Last night in the dream hunt, a huge, dark shadow crossed over them, casting fear into those running with her. The hounds disappeared, leaving her alone. The terror her hounds had experienced clung to her on waking. She wished she knew what it meant.

"Ouch!" Her scalp screamed in protest as Mica tugged on her hair. She pried it out of his grasp and put him back in his basket amid howls of protest. Esta came to investigate.

"I take it he pulled your hair again," Esta said, her brown eyes dancing with delight. She had never been as happy as she was since Samael, and now Mica, entered her life. Kat longed for such a simple existence, but Esta had endured tough times. Her sister once juggled being high lady of house Aranati with the life of a smuggler to keep her family and workers fed. And she had to fight for Sam's survival when he was sentenced to death for being a pirate. Yes, there had been hard times for Esta, and she deserved this peace. However, Kat couldn't help being a little jealous.

"He did! I think it's his favorite pastime. I must wear it up if he insists on pulling it." She combed her fingers through her dark hair. Esta's eyes narrowed.

"What's troubling you, Kat?"

Esta always saw through her front to the trouble within!

"It's nothing. I'm just tired."

"Is Hetty ill again?"

"No, she's fit as a horse. I spoke to her last night."

Esta shuddered. "I don't think I'll ever get used to you being able to speak to her through the fire. Did she give you unsettling news?"

"Nothing she revealed to me." Kat was sure something troubled Hetty, but the old woman was evasive even when asked direct questions. The main thing Kat was glad of was that Hetty was doing so well.

Esta sat in the chair beside her and picked Mica up from his basket to feed. "Speak, Sister."

Kat sighed. "I'm having dreams. They leave me uneasy, and, last night, there was a darkness I couldn't discern. It struck fear into my heart. I don't know what it means."

Esta frowned. "It may mean nothing."

Kat felt Esta only grudgingly accepted magic, let alone dreams which forebode trouble. Perhaps she should speak to Hetty. Or Alecia. The princess was rumored to herself have dreams that foretold the future.

Kat remained silent, but it didn't stop Esta.

"Are you happy? Since you returned from Brightcastle, you seem different. I know you suffer from melancholy, but this is …I don't know…You seem determined to stay busy, almost frantic. What happened while you were away? You never said."

"I helped bring Hetty back from certain death," Kat snapped, "and that's all that matters." She didn't wish to discuss her disappointments when she was trying to leave them behind her.

Esta shook her head. "I remember you telling me once I didn't trust you. And now you're doing the same thing. We're family, and I want you to tell me all your fears, even when you think I won't understand. What happened in Brightcastle?"

"This has nothing to do with Brightcastle."

"Doesn't it? Are you sure?" Esta asked. Mica fussed, and his mother sat him up and blew a raspberry on his neck which made him giggle.

Kat sighed. "Perhaps you're right. The Goddess knows I've carried this around with me for long enough." She didn't know where to start. "I met a man, I fell in love, and he rejected me."

Esta gasped. "Sam said a man was to blame, but I …I didn't think so. I wondered…"

"You thought I preferred women?" Kat stood. "How little you know of me."

"Who is he, Kat?"

"It doesn't matter. He's betrothed to another, and that's the end of it. He may already be married."

"Would it have been a good match? You and him?" Esta placed her son in his basket and stood. She grasped Kat's hands.

"It would have been more magical than all the spells in all the lands. When we touched, there was a wild current that tied us together. I gave him everything." Tears sprang into her eyes at the memory of what they had shared. "It wasn't to be, and I'm determined to move forward. My melancholy has vanished as mysteriously as it came, and I've tried hard to build a life for myself since returning."

"I've noticed, love," Esta said. "And I appreciate all you do. I wondered at the changes I saw. I thought perhaps Hetty…" She sighed and looked down at their joined hands. "Promise you'll ask for help when you need it. You're so solitary. It's not good for you." She kissed Kat's cheek, picked up her son, and left the room.

Kat gazed after her. If Esta only knew the whole story... night hounds and the rest. But her sister couldn't help. This was Kat's responsibility, her chosen vocation, and she would muddle through, feeling her way, because even Hetty might not be able to guide her.

That night, she dreamed of James. He was back in Costa, and an air of sadness hung over him. She watched him in his workshop, saw him meet with an old man, and take a note in exchange for coin. A raven squawked overhead then took flight. Even in the dream, she shivered. James looked at the sky and frowned. The images were jumbled, but the danger was clear. The sky seemed to hang dark, menacing, then out of the north came a strange sound. It was an almighty shriek, louder than a bird call, and a flight of ravens swept across the town, fleeing south. The shriek came again and dark, dark...

She sat up in bed, expecting to hear the sound. It was quiet with only her harsh breathing and frantic heartbeat to trouble the night. She drew deep breaths to settle the moths battering her stomach then rose from the bed and strode to the window. Dawn was only moments away. The full moon would rise tonight, and she and the hounds would hunt. A small thrill joined the dread within. What did it mean? She was certain something terrible would soon happen. Could she make sense of it all before it was too late?

* * *

James had spent the day mired in what his life had become over the last five months - since his rejection of Katrine Aranati. Where was she? What was she doing? He had enquired before leaving Brightcastle four months ago, and Hetty told him she was long gone. But gone where? Their last encounter had been momentous, and Katrine seemed to command the hounds which was difficult for him to accept. Her world was so foreign. Yet, she had taken up residence in his thoughts, and there was no shifting her. He wondered if she thought of him at all.

Yesterday at the inn he'd made a pledge. He would no longer drink to excess. But the temptation had been there today, luring him out to the inn to partake in a swift ale that might become ten if he wasn't careful. This evening, he had won the battle, and his day had been more productive than most. He was almost finished the tiara, and soon he could deliver it to Princess Benae. He wondered what reception he'd get after the debacle of his betrothal. Melanis and Benae, if not close friends, at least saw each other often.

He sighed. That was a worry for another day. He locked the front door and went to check the back before turning in. As he reached it, the hairs on the back of his neck stood up. He opened the door and stepped out, lifting the lantern he carried. A full sweep of the yard showed nothing out of order.

A hen shrieked, and he jumped. He puffed out a breath and checked his knives before grabbing the wooden pole that rested inside the door. It should be protection enough from the mangy dog or fox in his hen house. Why hadn't Lamb given the alarm? Stupid big lump of dog was probably curled up in the shed asleep.

James closed the door and ventured into the yard. He peered inside the shed - Lamb wasn't there. Feathers fluttered on the ground outside the henhouse, but all was quiet.

Except for the low grinding.

It sounded like…sounded like…a dog chewing on a bone. He looked up toward the noise and spied a dark lump on the roof of his house. A huge lump…no…a *massive* lump. His heart slowed to a limp, and his mouth dried. Thick liquid dripped from the roof.

As he charged for the safety of the house, the dark blob lifted and swooped straight at him. Huge scale-covered claws with razor-sharp talons knocked him to the ground. Lamb's head fell beside him as the creature swept by. He rolled onto his back, brandishing the pole and the lantern, seeking the beast. The lantern light hindered his night vision, but he wasn't ready to discard it when he might need the fire.

It took two sweeps of the surrounding buildings before he found his attacker sitting atop his neighbor's house. The moon came out from the clouds to reveal the huge ugly head of…a *dragon*? Its eyes glinted crimson, and, for a moment, James couldn't move. The beast shifted, its claws sliding on the roof. A tile slid to the alley, and a cat screamed. James stood and backed toward the house where Lamb's lifeblood dripping from the roof made a sticky curtain between him and the back door. The dragon flapped its wings as though to launch, but he'd be inside before the cumbersome beast could reach him.

At that moment, Dant stepped from the stable.

"What's all the noise?" He saw James. "Oh, sorry Master."

"Get back inside!" James charged across the yard toward the stable hand. "Dragon!"

Dant stared at him as though he'd gone mad.

"Get inside, I say!" James spared a look over his shoulder. The beast launched from its perch and flapped toward them. "Run!"

James set himself ready to knock the beast aside with the pole. Then it was above him, the reek of its breath alone enough to bring bile to his throat. He choked and swung the pole, not connecting with anything. He swung back the other way at the hovering beast. This close, he could see the intelligent eye of the dragon. It was waiting for him to drop his guard.

Keeping eye contact, he put down the pole and picked up the lantern. Give the beast a dose of its own fire! But perhaps fire didn't scare it, for it charged at James. He flung the lantern, and then it was upon him. One clawed foot seized his left shoulder and the other his knee. Agony laced through him, and he realized he only had one chance to live. He pulled the knife from his belt and sliced upward, gouging a deep cut in the beast's right forearm. It dropped him and flapped away, a massive gout of flame shooting across the yard and into the neighboring houses as it let out a scream.

And then the beast again turned its baleful eye on James. He braced himself and drew back his right arm to throw the knife. Perhaps he could get in a killing shot before the dragon's flaming breath consumed him. But, as he threw his knife, a fireball blazed across the yard and hit the beast in the side. Another one followed, and the dragon launched itself into the night sky, its wing on fire as it flapped out of sight.

* * *

Kat dropped to the dirt of the yard and ran to James's side. He was bleeding from his left shoulder and knee where the beast had seized him.

"Katrine! What…"

"Hush, don't talk. We must get you inside." She looked for Dant. "Help me!"

Together, they got James inside and to his bed. The house next door was on fire, and, already, the neighboring residents had set up a bucket line to help put it out.

Kat seized Dant by the shoulders. "Fetch my horse from the street and stable him. Then gather all the staff and help with the fire. Tell them your master is ill."

She returned to James.

"What are you doing here, Lady?" he said. "I thought never to see you again."

She used her knife to cut his trousers, so she could examine his knee wound, then removed his tunic and shirt. "You hoped never to see me again, you mean? Where's your wife?"

"It's a long story."

She stared. "You *are* married?"

"I am not. Look, my wounds are burning like they're on fire. Could we leave this until later?"

She bit back the words she longed to batter him with and inspected both of his wounds. "They're deep. I think they'll fester."

"I have every faith in your healing ability."

"You're a fool!" She turned and left the room.

In the kitchen, Kat found a kettle with recently boiled water and several bowls. She prepared a herb solution and took it back to the bedroom. James had closed his eyes but opened them as she cleaned the skin around his wounds.

"This will hurt, but you must bear it." She gave him a knife handle to bite down on. "Whatever happens, you mustn't move. I'll open your wounds so I can flush them out."

So saying, she seized the knife she had placed in the kitchen fire and plunged it into his shoulder. James screamed as if dying, and Kat almost lost the courage to continue. *I must do this, or he will die!* She swallowed down the lump that had lodged in her throat and listened to Hetty's voice in her head. *"Open the wound until you fear it will never heal. It's only then you've cut deep enough."* She discovered bruised flesh extending beyond the cut and braced herself to slice again.

He screamed, but not as loudly as the first time. Blood poured from the deepened cut, and she feared he might die of blood loss. She needed to treat this wound first and stem the blood flow before she moved to his knee. James had gone quiet, his breathing shallow and fast.

She flushed the wound, and the bleeding subsided until the solution leaving the wound was almost clear. The herbs must have aided in stemming the blood flow; or he had lost so much blood he had none to spare.

Her hands shook so hard she could hardly hold the needle to suture the gaping hole. At least James wasn't suffering, unconscious as he was. Perhaps she could complete her surgery before he awoke. She placed the last stitch and wiped the wound clean, then moved to his knee. Blessedly all the punctures appeared to have avoided the joint itself. There were three, and she opened all of them without a murmur from her patient. Kat flushed until the fluid ran clear again and closed the cuts. Then she cleaned up and settled down in a chair to wait.

When Kat awoke with a stiff neck the next morning, James still lay unmoving. She hurried to his side and checked his skin. He was warm but not feverish, his face pale not flushed. If the wounds had festered it would be obvious by now. But he wouldn't wake, and fear sat like a cold stone in her heart and gut.

What if she had killed him with her surgery? She drew a deep breath and turned to place more wood on the fire. She couldn't give up until there was no more reason to hope.

All through the morning, Kat waited. She took her breakfast in his room, delivered by the housekeeper, Mistress Lary. The house next door had been saved, and no one was aware how the fire had started but for her, Dant and James. The stable hand told Mistress Lary James had been attacked by a wolf, and Kat saw no reason to tell her otherwise. *She* still couldn't accept what she had seen. The last dragon had vanished over a hundred years ago, yet one had attacked the household last night. Why? Had it been sent by someone?

It was rumored the dragons of old were raised by elves. Was this another plot by the rebel faction of dark elves to subdue the kingdom? She had seen no rider, but dragons were rumored to be intelligent. Perhaps this one had been trained to spy on Costa. What if she hadn't acted on her fears and raced to check that James was well? What if her dreams hadn't warned her of a dark shadow of peril hanging over him?

James had fought valiantly, but was ill prepared to battle a dragon. She wanted to believe he would have escaped with his life even without her magic. Her heart swelled at the memory of his fight with the huge beast. James had never given up! But she had to acknowledge he had been seconds from being toasted by dragon fire.

Night hounds and, now, dragons. At least the hounds appeared to be under her control, but the dragon? Never… How many more of them were hiding out there? She closed her eyes and sat back in a chair by the window. It would be luncheon soon, and James must wake before long. It was only a matter of time.

CHAPTER 16

JAMES opened his eyes to flickering candlelight. Where was he? On the road? In his room? He fought a foggy memory which must be a dream - a dragon had grabbed him and tried to fly away? He huffed out a breath and pain blazed from his left shoulder. Agony scorched up his neck, across his chest, and down to the tips of his fingers. And he was ravenous.

He turned his head to the side. There he saw another illusion. *Katrine.*

The glimmer of candlelight danced on her hair and face. She was the most beautiful thing he had ever laid eyes on. Wait…it was no dream! She had come in the nick of time to save him from the dragon. She was everything he had ever believed she was - brave, strong and true. Shame struck him at the way he had chosen Melanis over her. Both were fine women but…

His head battled his heart. He generally listened to his head. It was the way to keep the world under control. It was how you made the right decisions and created order. None of those concepts resonated with him at this moment as he looked upon Katrine.

And then she opened her eyes and stared straight at him. The brilliance of her eyes struck him, and he couldn't look away. It seemed she was imprinting herself in his memory, to always be connected to him. He was helpless to break the link.

She stood and stretched, giving him another chance to admire her.

"How do you feel?" she asked, approaching like a wary cat.

"Like a dragon picked me up and dropped me, then someone sliced into me with hot knives," he said. "Please tell me I dreamed all of it."

She frowned and placed a cool hand on his forehead. "It was no dream." She let out a long breath. "Still no fever. I think you might survive." She sat on the edge of the bed and placed her head in her hands.

"I didn't realize my survival would upset you so."

She dropped her hands and turned to him. James flinched at the raw pain on her face - the exhaustion, and the shadows. "Stop being so flippant and be real with your emotions. I thought you'd die with only my poor skills to save you. You don't understand how it felt - to fear, to be sure I wasn't good enough. If you died…" She pushed off the bed and strode away to stand before the fire.

"It would never be your fault if I died."

She turned to him, fury in her spectacular eyes. "I would blame myself! And, do you know, James. I don't think I could survive that." She turned away. He had never felt so cut off from her. How could he reach out to this woman who held the power to give him everything he never realized he needed.

He was at sea, had hurt her, perhaps too deeply to be forgiven. "How can I make my peace with you?"

Her shoulders slumped, but she kept her back to him. "I'm not sure if I wish for peace between us. It seems a foreign concept when our friendship has been so stormy."

Ah, at least she hasn't shut me out completely. He took a deep breath that set his shoulder throbbing. "Come here. Let me see your face." At least then he might understand her.

She advanced, like a wild creature, scared and hurt once, not daring to trust again. "I should leave you to rest."

"Damn it! This is more important than rest! I need to explain my actions."

She shook her head. "*You* need! Is it too much to ask that you consider what *I* need? Between us it has always been about you. *You* didn't like my sister, *you* decided I needed protection, *you* couldn't risk a relationship with me, and *you* were already *betrothed*. You... you... you! Well, forgive me if I don't want to be with a man who doesn't consider my wishes before his own."

James allowed her words to make their mark. He held her gaze as the shame burned. "I'm sorry."

Her eyes widened. "Is that all? 'I'm sorry'."

"It's a start, Katrine. I want to explain, and I wish to start afresh in our relationship - whatever it becomes. Though I hope for more than mere friendship."

She closed her eyes, her jaw clenched, and when she opened them again, she walked away. "You don't know how I wanted to hear those words. And now, when you say them, I'm no longer sure what I want. I'm strong, James, and I like the woman I've become."

He sensed her slipping away. He no longer knew her - that was the truth. She was stronger than the old Katrine, toughened in flames, hardened by his rejection.

She turned back to him. "You've made me strong in more ways than just my heart. Your rejection that day made me so angry I lost all fear for that one moment, and, in those few seconds, the hounds found me. I looked them in the eye without fear, and they accepted me. Now I lead them. They go where I go, and I have plans - real plans - for them. There is danger coming, and my hounds will have a part to play in the defense against that evil."

Her words struck fear into his heart. It was worse than he had thought. She was a witch and, now, the mistress of those dogs. What other surprises lay in her future? "And you're asking me to accept all of it?"

She gave a brief shake of her head. "I'm telling you what I am now. I don't need you to protect me." Her throat clenched as though the words were hard to say. It gave him hope that, though she didn't need him, her life may be better with him in it.

"Katrine, please, pull up a chair and listen."

She stood for a time, her eyes pinned to his, as if trying to dig out all his secrets. Then she did as she was bid. When she was seated, he began.

"After you left Brightcastle, I tried to tell myself it was for the best. I was committed to Melanis, and you to your magic. Those moments with you in the field didn't leave with you, Katrine. I dreamt of them night and day, and, instead of becoming less frequent, I saw you spread before me more often. When I tried to make love to my fiancée, it was your face I saw and your skin I touched. Then I opened my eyes and saw Melanis, and my body rebelled. I couldn't complete the act with her once I had you."

She made to stand and move away, but he held her there.

"I don't want to hear that woman's name," she protested.

"You need to. I've been with her for two years, and she was awaiting our official betrothal for almost half of that time. We were perfect for one another. But there was no love. It was the way I thought I wanted it. It was the only way I knew to bring a wife and children into my life without losing control. The thought of all the chaos that would normally follow a love match was abhorrent."

He held her attention if the intensity of her stare was anything to go by.

She reached for his hand. "I begin to understand, but is control of your life so important? Isn't a true and burning love so much more fulfilling?"

"It's important to *me*. The desire to control my world has motivated each decision I've made as an adult. Over the years, my obsession with order became a disease until I couldn't abide anything in my life not designed by me..."

"And then *I* ran into you that day and upset your neat and tidy world."

"Yes, and brought more danger than I've ever known. Suddenly, I was fighting night hounds, and escorting you to Brightcastle, and finding out you're a witch. You're the opposite of all I've planned for."

"Fate brought me to you," she whispered. "Perhaps the Goddess understands what you need better than you do."

"You don't change habits overnight when they've stood you in good stead all your adult life."

She cupped his cheek in her free hand. "Has your life been so perfect?"

James growled. This was not going as planned. "Hush while I explain." She frowned at him but stayed silent.

"I realized I couldn't be the man Melanis needed, so I broke off our engagement and left the city soon after. I returned to Costa and tried to put it all behind me."

"Did you succeed?"

James thought of the sad state his life had become over the last four months and shook his head. "I've been trying to get on with my life, throw myself back into work, look after my staff, and see my friends. But all I see when I close my eyes is you. Night and day, you're all I think of. I've not enjoyed an uninterrupted night's sleep in weeks. And I'm drinking more than I should."

"You do look wretched," she said, laying her palm on his forehead. "But at least the dragon wounds haven't festered. You should be able to resume your duties in a matter of weeks."

"And you?"

"I shall return to my estate when you no longer need me."

"Then you'll never return because I've decided I need you, forever."

Her eyes widened, and the silver flecks in them danced and spun. She blinked. "That sounds like a marriage proposal."

He pondered then nodded. "It was. Please stay with me and be my wife. We'll play it any way you like, only don't leave me."

Hope shone in her eyes but soon died. "I thought no one would ever want me," she whispered.

"What do you say to my proposal?"

She came out of a trance to spear him with her brilliant stare. "Does this mean you love me? Or am I merely a more palatable partner than Lady Stenmore?"

James wasn't ready for undying love declarations. Hell, he'd only just realized he needed Katrine in his life, let alone had time to examine the intricacies of his feelings. He only knew he had to have her, love her, and worship her. "I think I might be in love with you."

Her eyes narrowed. "You *might* be in love? It's not enough when I love you with each tiny particle of my being. I've known at least since the first time you rejected me, perhaps before. You must feel more for me than physical attraction. I must be everything to you. But, more than that, you must embrace the life that comes with me - magic, night hounds, and perhaps war."

It sounded dangerous when she put it like that, but he wasn't averse to danger. He was, after all, a spymaster, risking himself daily to collect and decode messages and pass them onto the king. But now wasn't the time to tell her that. Best to win her over before he revealed the rest of his secrets.

"I'm ready," he declared. "I've been miserable without you, thinking I'd never again have you in my life. And now you've rescued me from certain death. Yes, I must love you."

She made an indelicate noise through her nose. "Stop it. You don't know your own heart, James, so I won't marry you. I'll stay until you can fend for yourself and then return to my family." She got up and left the room.

He hadn't expected that. Stupid conceited man that he was, he hadn't thought she might turn him down. He imagined she must be as bereft as he was. But she had moved on with so much dignity. She had changed since Brightcastle, toughened, come into her own. While he diminished. It had to stop. He must have her, and he'd do whatever it took to bring her back to him, to love forever.

* * *

Kat cared for her patient even though every fiber of her being needed to flee. Every hour, she fell a little more in love. Each day, as she bathed his wounds, she worked harder to keep her touch professional. James had a body many men would kill for and every woman she knew would admire. He was an enigma, and she was sure he still hid secrets. She could not agree to marriage with him when he wasn't being honest with her.

What she needed was distance to think, not to be in his company day in and day out. A week had passed, and Kat believed in another few days she could saddle Demon and be gone. She would speak to Hetty and her sister and make a decision in her best interests. But would James be safe after she left? Might the dragon return to finish its work? At least whilst here, she could ensure he was well and lend a hand if the dragon came back.

But her sanity crumbled. She barely slept at night, knowing he was in the house. Her body was a wreck of desire, and if they happened to touch by accident, she almost leaped out of her skin. She paused in the grinding of her herbs with mortar and pestle. She had almost enough prepared so she could leave him well stocked for the rest of his recovery. If she stayed with James until he was up and about, she might never leave.

She returned from the kitchen with his luncheon meal and stopped dead inside the bedroom door. "What are you doing out of bed?"

Her voice was harsh, but he turned with ease from the stretch he was performing. She licked her lips at the way his shoulder muscles moved. *Not professional at all.* He faced her, and she swallowed at the sight of stomach muscles that had hardly softened with lack of use.

"I was going crazy in bed," he said. "Best I be up and moving. I think I'm ready."

"You should let me be the judge," she snapped, as she carried his meal to a small table by the window. She turned and stood facing him with her arms crossed over her chest.

His grey eyes raked her as if he was seeing her anew. "I can tell when I'm recovered enough. It's my body after all." He walked a few steps, still limping. "This knee should warm up nicely. Just needs a few steps across the room." He walked past her to the far corner and back, his limp improving with each step.

"Well then," she said, "it's time for me to return home if you no longer need me."

He stopped before her, close enough to touch, but after a week of her fending him off, he knew better. "Stay."

She looked away. "You know I can't."

"I know no such thing. I proposed to you a week ago, and you said 'no'. I ask again - please stay with me and be my wife."

She blew out a long breath. "I don't think you want me for a wife. You don't know what you want, except a peaceful life - and you won't get it with me."

He grasped her elbows, but she kept her arms crossed before her. *Don't encourage him!*

"Katrine, I thought I had explained how I felt. I'm obsessed with you. There's no one like you. Come live here with me, and we'll work the rest out. Bring your dogs. I don't care, only please say yes!"

She closed her eyes and up popped the image of him arching over her, pounding into her, giving her more joy than she had ever believed possible. Could he accept her for what she was? He said the words, but *could* he be the man she needed him to be? Or would he regret being tied to her magic and her world?

"James," she said, opening her eyes. "I'm not sure if you love me. Only you can decide. I want you to know one thing. I. Love. You. Whatever happens between us, I love you and always will."

"That sounds like 'goodbye'," he said, his hands tightening on her arms.

"That's exactly what this is. You're well enough for me to leave, and that's what I'm doing."

"You just admitted you love me."

"I do. And I'd give anything to be your wife, but I won't say 'yes' until I think you mean it. You must prove you love me, and you understand what loving me means. I know you've lived it, but you must be ready for this for the rest of your life. Forever."

"I—"

"No," she said, raising her hand, "I have no more to say. It's up to you. Please be careful. The dragon is still out there, and we don't know what it wants." She kissed his cheek, taking one last breath of his musky scent, and left the room.

CHAPTER 17

TWO weeks passed. To Kat, getting through each day was like crawling through quicksand. There was plenty to do on the estate as well as a young baby to mind. But the many mundane tasks left her mind free to contemplate what she had turned down.

James. He was with her each moment of every day and most of the night. He walked her dreams and made love to her over and over. Each time, she grew more frantic. Most mornings she awoke all hot and bothered, the sheets twisted into a snarled mess with her tossing and turning. This morning was no different, but at least the dragon was gone from her nightmares and those of the hounds.

She didn't regret her decision. James had hurt her with his rejection. Had pursued her and taken her virginity, and then disrespected her by asking her to take the tea that could prevent a pregnancy. He hadn't wanted her then, and now he had changed his mind. Would he change it again? When times became tough, and he struggled with the reality of life with her, would he honor her then? Or might he run away to another, less complicated woman?

She couldn't wait for him to prove himself, but must keep moving forward and hope missing him would get easier. So far, it wasn't the case. But, as much as she ached for him, the melancholy was gone for good. She was strong and fierce and would live a happy and successful life, with or without him.

"Kat! Hurry up! We need your trunk."

She stopped her daydreaming and threw the last of her garments into the chest. She shook the creases out of her skirt then ran her hands down over her bodice, pleased at the way the crimson gown hugged her curves. A small kernel of excitement spiraled up her spine. They were to attend the autumn ball at the palace!

Never usually one for dancing and dressing up, this time Kat had agreed to attend with her sister. Their Aunt Paurella, her mother's younger sister, was the Queen's Dressmaker, and she had created gowns for them. Esta and Sam were having their first formal social occasion as husband and wife, and Esta had quivered with anticipation for weeks.

The footman came for her chest, and she followed him from the house, stopping to say goodbye to her mother.

"Goddess preserve us!" Esta said, her head stuck out the Aranati coach window.

"You're finally here!"

"Are you really so excited at the prospect of dancing with your husband?" Kat asked as Sam handed her up into the coach. "Thank you, Sam." She sat and arranged her skirts, finding the billowing material unwieldy. *When did I last wear a gown?* It might be fun to be a lady again, as long as she kept her eyes downcast. Watch the gentlemen run if they glimpsed the silver flecks in her blue irises.

James always looked me in the eye.

"Oh, I am," Esta said. "I can't wait for the ball tomorrow and sharing this experience with you makes it all the more enjoyable. It will be like your season."

Kat laughed. "A short season indeed." She combed her long nails through her black hair, which was restrained in a crimson head band. Her nails were painted silver rather than purple, in deference to the more subdued environment of court.

Esta snared her hand. "Don't fret, dear. Sam and I will see you're treated with respect. And Nikolas too for that matter." She spoke of Sam's half-brother, Admiral Nikolas Cosara.

"I'm not concerned," she said, "and I can take care of myself." She couldn't admit it to Esta, but she was a little nervous about the ball and being at court. Give her the open sea or a deep forest any day over the idiots that frequented Wildecoast. But perhaps there were gentlemen with whom she might spend an enjoyable moment or two.

"Good," Esta said, "but none of the…" She wiggled her fingers in a magical way. "We have enough gossip about our family without adding more. Stick to safe topics like the weather and…how proud you are to be an aunty."

Kat smiled. "That I can do." She relaxed back in the seat and watched the countryside go by, shoving all thoughts of James out of her head. Tomorrow would be an occasion to remember!

Their arrival in Wildecoast, and the subsequent flurry of activity and dress fittings, had Kat's mind in a place that threatened to send her screaming into the sea. Finally, dressed in her cobalt blue satin gown and bedecked with silver and sapphires, Kat took a moment to enjoy a cup of chamomile tea in a quiet corner of Esta's suite of rooms. Her sister was still fussing and primping as if anyone would care if there was a hair out of place or a crease in her fern green gown.

Kat closed her eyes and tried to bring her erratic nerves under control. It was only a ball. It mattered not who was there or what they said of her. She would survive the night and keep her eyes down. Samael had promised her a dance and so had Nikolas. Surely the dancing lessons she had endured as a young girl would come back to her and stop her falling over her feet?

"I'm ready!" Esta announced, and Kat's heart flipped over in her chest. She took a great gulp of tea and choked on it, only just avoiding spraying the liquid over her skirt.

"Really, Kat," Esta said, handing her a handkerchief. "You must be more careful. Please don't go gulping your drink tonight!"

Kat placed her cup and saucer on the table and stood with as much dignity as possible after choking. "Don't worry, I'll do my best not to disgrace the family."

A knock at the door heralded Sam, who had dressed in another room to give the ladies more space. "Ready?" he asked, his green eyes gleaming as he took in the splendor of his wife. "You both look exquisite!"

His eyes never left his wife. Kat longed for a man to treasure her as Sam did Esta. She sighed, trying and failing to push the face of a certain master jeweler out of her mind.

"Let's get this over with." She sailed past Esta and Sam as they stood gazing at one another like two lovesick youngsters.

Kat fell into step behind her sister and brother-in-law as they made their way down to the ballroom. She groaned as she saw the dancers crowding the room. They were clearly among the last to arrive which meant all eyes would be upon them.

"Lady Esta Aranati and her husband Samael Delacost," the Master of Ceremonies said. "And Lady Katrine Aranati."

"Always the afterthought," Kat muttered under her breath as she walked through the doorway into the ballroom.

Under cover of the flurry of people who flocked to speak with Esta and Sam, she looked around the room, seeing few people she knew. Her palms grew sweaty and her face heated. *Too many!* How was she to deal with all these pretentious lords and ladies?

They had been howling for Samael's blood a year ago, yet now they appeared eager to rub shoulders with him socially. They couldn't have forgotten his trial so soon, or the fact he had consorted with the faction of dark elves known as *Sis Lenweri*. But here they were, clucking around Esta and Sam as if they could reap some benefit.

Thank the Goddess no one suspected Esta of anything more than loving a pirate. Kat didn't relish any investigation into how they had met Samael Delacost, how their one-time smuggling led them into the pirate's path. She shivered as she imagined the repercussions of such a revelation.

"Are you chilled, Lady?"

Kat turned to find a good-looking sandy-haired gentleman in a charcoal gray velvet tunic standing before her.

"Tomas Henn at your service." The man swept into a bow.

She curtsied. "Katrine Aranati, My Lord," she said, keeping her eyes lowered.

"Yes, I know who you are. I courted your sister before her failed engagement. Had I realized there was a more beautiful sister yet to come, I would have bided my time."

"You're too kind," Kat said, "but I don't think my sister would appreciate your slight."

"Forgive me, Lady Katrine, I meant no harm with my clumsy compliment."

She nodded. "You're forgiven."

"I wondered if you might do me the honor of dancing with me."

Kat nodded again and Lord Henn swept her onto the floor. He was a skilled dancer, good natured when she trod on his toes, and strong enough to guide her smoothly to the next step. Kat was surprised to find she enjoyed their two dances.

"Thank you, Lady Katrine," he said as he led her to the buffet table. "May I have another dance later in the evening?"

"I shall look forward to it," she said, smiling at the floor. Kat sought a chair and sat down before she received another offer. She needed time to compose herself. How was she to get through the night without making eye contact with her dance partners?

Esta and Samael approached. "Have a dance with Sam while I get my breath, Kat."

Sam escorted Kat onto the floor, and she tried not to compare his strong arms with those of another. Again, she knew the pang of longing for a man who could match her fire and also shield her from harm. *Keep your mind on your brother-in-law!*

"I've been meaning to speak to you for some time now, Sam."

"Oh?"

"Yes…I haven't always been your advocate. When Esta fell in love with you, I wondered if she had lost her mind."

"Love is a kind of insanity, don't you think?"

Kat thought of her feelings for James, how they made no sense most of the time. "I suppose so. Anyway, I wanted you to know I respect the way you've looked after Esta and pulled your life into a semblance of respectability."

Sam laughed out loud, and Kat scowled.

"Oh, Kat, how you do give backhanded compliments! Well, let me tell you, I care not for respectability for myself, but I love Esta. I'd do anything for her. And I'm enjoying my new life. The only thing I crave is more time at home to enjoy it."

"You never have to fear for her or your son while you're at sea. We're used to taking care of each other."

"Meaning what?"

"As I said. We take care of our own."

"I hope you include me."

Kat studied him. "Perhaps one day, Sam. I don't think you're quite there yet."

His arms tightened around her.

"Your sister believes I'm good enough for her," he growled.

Kat cocked her head on an angle. "As you said, love is a kind of insanity."

They finished the dance in silence, and he led her back to Esta then left to fetch drinks.

"Are you enjoying yourself yet, Kat? It's heartening to see you conversing with Sam. I feared you might never make friends."

"We're friendly enough. And yes, I'm relaxing a little as the evening goes on. Tomas Henn seems to like me."

Esta smiled. "You could do worse than him, you know. He has not long inherited the family estate. You'd be a wealthy woman as his lady, and he has a certain appeal."

"And what if I don't wish to marry for money? What if I never marry at all?" She was beginning to think it was a definite possibility.

"As I told you before," Esta said. "You need not give up on marriage. Perhaps you could grow to love Lord Henn?"

She didn't want to discuss her love life, even with her sister. "Perhaps. Are you enjoying yourself?"

Esta beamed. "Oh, yes! I admit I was nervous about the reception Sam would get, but his connection to Nikolas seems to ensure he's at least treated with politeness. I don't care what they all say behind our backs."

"At least we liven up an event by our presence. As long as no one gets wind of how we made ends meet before you married Sam."

"Yes! I think we can breathe easily on that issue. With Nikolas on our side, there's no one else to ask questions." Esta looked around as the musicians played the first notes of a lively tune. "Where is Sam with our drinks? I wish to get back on the floor."

As she said the words, the king asked Esta for a dance, and Kat accepted a partner soon after. It was a fat lord who stood on her toes with each change of direction. The dance didn't last long and was followed by a flurry of different partners, leaving her breathless as the clock neared midnight.

She was thinking it might be time to retreat to her suite when there was movement on the stage. A tall dark-haired man in a mask stood before the musicians, his figure compelling her attention as the crowd hushed. As she stared, the man's eyes met hers across the crowded room. A spear of excitement struck her, and she tingled all the way to her toes. Who was he?

The music started, and he began to sing, rich tones pouring forth as he sang of thwarted love, of a lady in a tower who had spurned his offer of marriage, of his life now barren of anything worthwhile. Kat stood transfixed by his voice and those words! How did he understand how alone she felt since leaving James?

She stiffened and peered closer for the identity of the man as he sang the last chorus. His voice was hypnotic, deep and…familiar? Could it be James on stage? *What?*

The song ended, and the man stepped down to thunderous applause. He walked to Kat without ever taking his eyes off her and bowed.

"My Lady."

She curtsied, raising her eyes to his.

"James."

"You guessed."

Her body trembled so hard she could scarcely form words. "The song made me think of how I felt, and it gave me the clue. I didn't realize you sang."

"Neither did I until I dreamt up this idea."

"What do you mean?"

"After you left, I couldn't accept your decision not to marry me. I came up with a plan to win you back. It wouldn't be necessary if I had followed my heart in the first place. Forgive me. I never meant to hurt you. I hope my song made you understand where my heart now lies."

He brought her close to him, and it was her body's turn to sing as they danced a waltz. To have James this close again was heaven, but where her heart rejoiced, her head debated.

"I miss you too, James, only I can't help feeling you might change your mind when the reality of life with me takes hold. I have to know you're true."

"Doesn't this prove how serious I am?" He pushed his mask on top of his head, revealing eyes haunted with desperation. "It's a public declaration of my love."

"I know."

"Can't you forgive a stupid man for getting his priorities wrong?"

"James Tomel!" A dark-haired, bearded man with piercing blue eyes seized James by the shoulder. "What the hell do you think you're doing?" The man's fingers curled into James's coat like a claw. "You'll be a laughingstock in the guilds."

The man turned to Kat, his body held stiffly. "My Lady."

"Hello, Reid." She couldn't think what to say to the man Esta had promised to marry and then run out on. He must still be fuming. "I hope you're well."

Reid stared at her. "I'm getting on with business, which is more than I can say for James." His attention shifted back to his friend. "Have you taken leave of your senses, man?"

James drew himself up while Kat wished she could slink away and leave them to it.

"I thought I sounded quite good."

Reid snorted. "That's not what I meant, and you know it. You're making a fool of yourself *and* over the sister of a woman who broke her vow to me."

James held up a finger. "Watch your words, or I'll be forced to do something I shouldn't at a royal event."

She clutched James's arm. "Leave him be. We don't wish for a scandal."

James pulled her close and addressed Reid. "I love this woman, and I won't have you casting slurs on her name or her sister's."

There was a collective gasp from those nearby. They had gathered a crowd observing the unfolding drama. Kat wished even more for the quiet of her room.

"You idiot!" Reid's face glowed like the setting sun over the mountains on a warm summer day. "After I told you what I endured, you wish to be associated with this lady? You deserve every bad thing that comes to you." He turned and strode through the crowd, leaving whispers in his wake.

James escorted Kat from the floor and found a quiet alcove where he could shield her with his body.

"I'm sorry about Reid," he said. "I hope you realize I'd choose you over him in a heartbeat."

She looked up into the serious intensity of his gaze, all the while trying to make sense of what he was doing here. Should she give him what he sought?

"He's your friend. I don't expect you to turn your back on him. You shouldn't have to do that." And what if Reid discovered her talents? He'd shout it from the rooftops.

"I can deal with losing a friend, but I can't live without you. I've hurt you deeply in so many ways, but I think I can make you happy. Please say you'll marry me, and we'll find a priestess and make it official."

She stared. "This was a beautiful gesture, James, but it doesn't change anything. You think you want me, but I must be sure you know your own heart."

"I love you, dammit, and you feel deeply for me. I've seen it in your eyes, sensed it in your body, and felt it in your care when I was injured. Tell me you don't love me."

She watched his hope turn to despair as she allowed the silence between them to lengthen. "Sometimes it takes more than love to make a forever. You must prove you have it in you to trust me, and love me, and forgive me when my true essence is more than you can deal with."

"That's not fair. How can we know the future? All I know is I can't live without you. I hoped you felt the same."

She grabbed his lapels and pulled him close, planting a kiss on those lips that had stolen her heart. "I love you, but you have to understand, right now, I *can* live without you. I'm not the same woman you seduced in the meadow. I've climbed a mountain since then, and I can see so much more from the summit than before."

"What can I do?"

"Prove you can be my partner in all I do. I don't just need your love, I need your support, and tenderness, and forgiveness. I need your truth. If I give my heart fully to you, James, there will be no going back. You must be sure."

She pushed past him, refusing to look back as she fled to her suite.

* * *

James sat on his bed in a tavern in the best quarter of Wildecoast city. He hadn't even loosened his tie or taken off his coat. He'd been so damned sure Katrine would fall at his feet when he sang to her.

Anger simmered but he was trying to control it. Letting his temper run free was no way to make the next decision on what he could do to fix things with his love.

Was it fair of her to demand he prove himself? Surely, he had already done that? Yes, but you ruined it all, so now you must begin again. He had destroyed a precious gift when he spurned Katrine's love. And he couldn't make it right merely by saying sorry. But what else could he do? He'd put his reputation on the line performing at the ball tonight. Reid was right. He might well be the laughingstock of Wildecoast by tomorrow. And it was all for nothing.

Or was it? Katrine had kissed and touched him with tenderness. It was just a matter of finding the right path back to her.

Something she said stuck in his memory. *I need your truth*. What did she mean? Did she suspect he was still hiding things from her? She didn't know everything about him by a long way, whereas he knew all her deepest and darkest secrets - her eyes, her magic, the hounds… that she was a witch.

Did she suspect he harbored one last secret? His position as spymaster? He wasn't meant to divulge it to anyone but his informants. Did it matter if he revealed his clandestine career to Katrine? He was already withholding information from King Beniel that he should have passed on, principally Katrine's own secrets and the existence of the dragon.

James slammed his hand down on his thigh. Perhaps it was time to get out of the spy service and let a man whose heart was free take the risks. He didn't know if he had the stomach for it anymore.

CHAPTER 18

THE note came for Kat the next afternoon as she strode back and forth across Esta's sitting room. Her sister sat, patching a stocking and clucking at Kat's restless pacing.

"We will return to the estate tomorrow and not a moment sooner, Sister," Esta said. "I don't understand your urgency to leave. I should be the one pacing, missing Mica as I am."

Kat glared at her sister, then took the missive from a maid and waited until the woman left. Of course, Esta couldn't understand. She didn't have twenty-one hounds in her head, all longing to spend a night in her company. She broke the seal and unfolded the paper. It was from James. He requested her presence for supper that evening - at a tavern of all things, albeit in the private dining room. She told Esta.

"You must take an escort if you intend to meet. The Goddess only knows what gossip will result even accompanied by a chaperone."

"Perhaps I won't go. What can he say that will change things between us?"

"You won't know if you don't meet him," Esta said. "I thought last night's gesture was sweet. He took a grave risk, and his friendship with Reid must have been tested. You mean more to him than his friend or his business, or at least that's how I see it."

Kat considered. "Yes, when I first met James, he disliked me because I was your sister. It seemed then his relationship with Reid was of the utmost importance."

"Go and see what he has to say."

"Do you think Sam might escort me?"

"I'll ask him." Esta rang the bell for her maid.

Which was how Kat came to be seated with James in the cozy private dining room of The Laughing Dragon. Sam stood guard outside the door, and a young serving girl was at their beck and call.

"You have a remarkable sense of humor." Kat swirled the mulled wine in her goblet before taking a mouthful. "I thought you would do anything to avoid dragons."

James laughed. "It was recommended, and I couldn't ignore the irony. But I don't wish to talk about the dragon. I want to talk about our future."

Kat stared into the fire. "I don't see a future for us at the moment."

"Why? I can see you have deep feelings for me."

"Perhaps they're only feelings of desire, nothing deeper."

"It's not just that!" James stood and leant on the back of his chair.

"Keep your voice down, or Sam will be in here."

He took a deep breath as though trying to bring his temper under control.

"You said you needed to trust me. I invited you here to tell you something I should have revealed and didn't. Or perhaps I still shouldn't reveal, but need to, considering our relationship."

"You're not making any sense."

He paced across the room and back, his eyes darting about as though searching for escape. Finally, he stopped before her, his hands clasped in front. "I'm a spy."

Kat's heart gave a giant thud, the room around her jerking off kilter. James reached for her as she swayed in her chair. "What do you mean?" She had suspected James kept still more secrets even after she learned of his fiancée, but never had she imagined he harbored a secret second career. And as a spy!

"I'm actually a spymaster. I collect information from my contacts in Wildecoast, Costa, and Brightcastle, and convey it to the throne."

"What type of information?"

"Anything relevant to the security of the kingdom."

"My witchcraft could be, as well as the dragon." It was another nail in the coffin of their future. How could he contemplate marriage to her when this giant complication guided his life?

He nodded. "I would never expose you. As for the dragon, I need to decide what to do. The king must be told about the beast."

Her mind ran riot, imagining how James could reveal the dragon without divulging too much. How could they ever be together with him in a position that was directly opposed to her very existence? He would be compromised.

"We can never marry if you continue as spymaster, James."

His face turned pale, and a tremor ran through him. "It might be a difficult thing to walk away from." He paced again, talking as he walked. "I don't know if I *can* walk away. I know too much."

She grabbed his arm as he made to walk past. "Would your life be at risk?"

"I'd like to say no, but …"

"You might try to refuse the king and find yourself dead in an alley! Please tell me there is provision for those who no longer wish to serve!"

"I don't know anyone who has turned their back on this role," he hissed.

"Look at me," she said, rising from her chair and reaching for his hands. "This question requires an answer. I can't take you into my heart and my life if this will come between us. And it will, James. You know it. This secret is another reason I can't accept your proposal."

"So you'll allow my other life to thwart what we have? I treasure you beyond words." He clutched her to his chest, and his mouth descended on hers as though he were a starving man. There was no tenderness, only desperate passion, as his lips mastered all her resistance. She had longed for this those restless nights. Her body sang, her heart pounded with desire for this man who had made her a woman.

Her arms crept up his chest and around his neck to play with the long hair at his nape. She wove her fingers up the base of his skull, and the breath caught in his throat.

"I wish we could be together this night, beloved," he said. "I'd show you what you deny yourself."

"Don't you think I understand what I'm missing?" She closed her eyes, clawed her wits back to the moment, then gave him her full attention. "I remember our magic, James, I remember it well. I also recall what happened afterward."

She pulled back, hoping he might disagree but knowing he could not.

He gripped her forearms. "I'd do anything to turn back time, to repair the hurt I did to you. I can't. I must move forward and hope you can one day forgive me."

She sighed. James was difficult to deny when he stood before her, rubbing her skin with his callused thumbs. It was exquisite torture. She longed for him body and soul. Why shouldn't she have all he offered?

"I fear we'll never be together. Perhaps we can exist on fleeting moments like this which would torture us more than nurture. I don't think I could stand walking away after each encounter. Could you?"

He frowned at her. His shoulders slumped, and all the passion of a moment ago fled in the cold light of reality.

"I must go," he said. "But know this. I'll never give up on us." He drew her close. "I *will* find a way, and, when I do, your only choice will be to say 'yes'." He kissed her with a fierce longing then wrenched his lips from hers and left the room.

* * *

The darkness welled up in James as he walked the streets determined not to enter an inn and drink to forget. His lips burned from his last fierce contact with Katrine, and his body hummed with unsated desire.

How had his world gone so askew from the ordered existence it had been before she barreled into him?

His whole life focus had changed from work and order to love and chaos. He didn't welcome the turmoil, but he yearned for Katrine. He suspected her love would make the chaos worthwhile. Nothing else would matter.

Did she feel anything as deeply as he did? When he kissed her, she responded with passion. How then could she refuse his proposal? He had crushed her; it was all he could reason. The hurt led to mistrust of her instincts and of him. And although he confessed to his hidden life, it had only made things far worse. Perhaps he should've kept his mouth shut? He should have continued his espionage and not told Katrine. She would've been safer in ignorance. But that was no way to start a marriage!

Damn the circles his mind was taking! He had never been uncertain before this woman scrambled his brain, made him want things he had never desired - like love. His current dilemma was exactly why he craved order, and now order was gone forever. Katrine had pushed her way into his heart and possessed it.

How could he bring about a resolution? He must persuade her to take a chance. She would never regret it, but how could he convince her? They could work the rest out - the magic, the hounds, his secret career, and the danger - all of it.

CHAPTER 19

KAT'S mood was low as she, Esta and Sam left Wildecoast for home. One part of her longed to get back into the normal routine of the estate and stay busy. At least then she might put thoughts of James from her mind. Her heart lurched at the memory of his kisses last night and at the realization she may have enjoyed her last embrace with the man who had awakened her. She groaned softly.

"What's the matter?" Esta asked. "You made a strange sound then."

She turned from the window to look at her sister. "I was thinking of all the chores awaiting us at home."

Esta laughed. "You've been quiet since your dinner with James. I'll bet it's him you're thinking of. His eyes, his arms, and his—"

"Esta!" Kat's face radiated heat. Her sister was so tactless at times, too indelicate for the head of an estate. It was amazing how being married had changed her. Might it do the same for Kat too? She already felt transformed since her experiences with James, and she longed to explore more of her sexual side. But pleasuring herself was the closest she would come to sex. Unless she took a lover. The idea held no interest.

"Seriously, Kat! The man seems perfectly suitable. He's the head of his guild, for goodness sake. He's handsome and fit, and he seems to adore you. I don't understand what's holding you back."

"He's all those things, but he chose another woman and dallied with me, though he was unofficially betrothed. It's not something I can forget. He can't flip and flop between women as he chooses."

Esta regarded her with warm brown eyes full of understanding. "I appreciate how one can trap themselves into that circumstance. I committed my life to Reid even though I was falling fast for Sam." She reached for her husband and rested her hand on his cheek. They gazed into each other's eyes for a moment.

"Matters of the heart are not so easily settled, Kat," Esta continued. "This relationship James had with his lady was of long standing, and he didn't expect the love of his life to come along and upset all his carefully laid plans."

"You make it sound simple, and it's not."

"It's as simple as saying 'yes'. I want you to be happy with a man you yearn for more than anything else in this world. I think James is the right man."

Kat turned back to the window and watched the farmland roll by. An object in the distance caught her attention. Something white. As she drew closer, she spied a bouquet of white roses and asked the coachman to stop. A note was attached to the stunning flowers.

Forgive me. You'll never regret it. All my love, James.

She climbed back on board with the bouquet, and Esta squealed.

"Where did he find flowers like this?" she asked. "It's one of the most romantic gestures I've ever witnessed."

Sam smiled from his seat. "I may have given him a little help."

Esta hugged him while Kat hid her face in the bouquet, drinking in the perfume she had always adored but enjoyed only on the rarest of occasions. Tears welled, a lump caught in her throat, and her traitorous heart shoved against the bindings she had wrapped around it.

She was reminding herself of all the reasons she and James couldn't be together when, next, a posy of red roses appeared, tied to a fence post at the side of the road. The note with it said:

Marry me, Katrine, and you'll make me the happiest man
in the kingdom.

"He knows how to make the grand gestures," Esta said, as Kat climbed back on board. "Did you help with this one too, Sam?"

He smiled. "I like the man, and I want to see Kat happy. I agree with you, my love. They make a good pair."

"I'm right here in the carriage with you," she said, glaring at them and regretting her recent uncharitable treatment of Sam. "It's not that simple. The roses are a nice touch, but two bunches of flowers will *not* tip the balance." White roses were unusual, but the red were so rare that Kat had never actually seen them let alone been given a bouquet. She steeled her heart against the gesture - after all, what were roses when measured against a lifetime of commitment?

They continued until they were almost home. Kat couldn't believe what she saw tied to the estate arch. Red and white roses were intertwined across the arch, and a red satin cushion lay on the ground below the decoration. On it rested a white satin box. Kat's heart beat fast as she alighted and stood before the cushion. When she glanced over her shoulder, Esta and Sam were watching from the coach, grinning from ear to ear.

Kat let out a long sigh and bent to retrieve the box. When she flipped open the top, a stunning silver engagement ring, complete with a large blue sapphire the exact color of her eyes, sparkled back at her.

The breath left her body and refused to return. As the edges of her vision turned black, Kat gulped a breath and stood, hands trembling. The ring, nestled within its box, glared up at her as if all her life depended upon it. Prickles of fear skittered up the back of her neck. It was too much to take in. The trouble he had gone to…he was serious, and she was in no state to make this decision.

She snapped the box shut and shoved it into her bosom, then kicked the cushion into the bushes at the edge of the arch.

"Drive on," she snapped at the coachman, then turned and stalked ahead of the coach right up to her front door. James must be here, awaiting her answer. Well, she'd give him a piece of her mind for assuming so much as to leave her an engagement ring. She had told him how it stood between them, and he ignored everything she said!

She barged through the door, startling the maid who was about to answer it.

"James…James!" She called his name while searching the estate house, opening every door in the place. "Where are you hiding?" She entered her mother's room, breathing hard.

"Where is he?"

Lady Aranati senior peered at her over her sewing. "Where is who, dear? More like 'where are your manners'?"

Kat fought down a caustic remark and bent to kiss her mother's cheek. "Hello, Mother."

She stood, shifting her weight from one foot to the other. "I'm looking for Master James Tomel. You must have met him. He's been to the estate. Even he daren't ride by without stopping in to pay his respects."

"Oh! Yes, Master Tomel. He stayed to luncheon and has only just left." Her mother patted her hair as if recalling complements paid to her. "What a nice young man, and so accomplished. He seemed rather fond of you, Katrine. He asked me to forward his regards to you, and your sister and brother-in-law."

Kat's shoulders slumped. "Why did he leave me gifts and depart before I could speak to him?"

"If you don't mind me saying, my dear, you can be rather caustic; even downright rude."

Kat rested her hands on her hips. "He's a coward. And he won't take no for an answer!"

Her mother stood. "Hold your tongue. I can't think why you would criticize him. He cares deeply for you. If you ask my advice, I urge you to find him and accept his proposal."

"So! You know all about his sneaky tactics! He has been here trying to influence you, show you his good properties while leaving me a trail of gifts he imagines I can't say no to. Well, if he thinks I'll cave in for a pretty ring and some roses, he has another thing coming!" She turned to leave the room, but Esta stepped in and closed the door firmly behind her. A tremor ran through Kat's body, and tears welled. Damn her emotions! Why must she always cry when she was angry?

"Please don't be cross," Esta said, her warm brown eyes infuriating Kat more because she so rarely lost her composure. "James loves you, and he's a good man. If you spurn him, you'll regret it."

Kat lifted her nose in the air. "This is between James and me, not my whole family. You made a bad enough mess of your own romance with Sam."

"And that's why I can't see you throw away your chance at happiness. Things have been difficult for you. There were times in the past when I feared you wouldn't return from one of your trips, when I thought you didn't care if you lived or died."

Kat's stomach clenched at her words and shame swirled up to choke her. She had felt like that for months, had pulled herself through life without joy or direction until the day in the meadow. Making love with James and being spurned had unleashed a potential within her that she thought was burned out in the Crystal Cave. And then her white-hot anger on learning of his betrothal had sealed her recovery. She had him to thank for searing away her sadness and replacing it with determination. She'd never return to despair, not now she had found this new strength, this fresh purpose.

Esta continued. "Since James came along, you're strong and determined…you even smile now and then. Don't turn your back on him, Kat. You and he could be a formidable team, and he could make you happy."

"I don't need him to make me happy. I thought I did, but I've remade myself like a newly forged sword. You don't know the half of what I am."

Esta's eyes widened. "What do you mean?"

"I've grown as a sorceress and even more as a woman. Within me is all I'll ever need to be happy and successful. But the less you know of the sorcery the better."

"But you've told James?"

Kat nodded. "I've revealed all there is to know about me – there's nothing that can defeat us from my side. But I'm not so sure about James. *He* has been like an onion, peeling back the outer shell to find another hidden entity below. There's no telling what else he has to reveal."

"What if there's nothing?" Esta asked. "What if your suspicions kill the love you share?"

Kat shook her head. "You don't understand. Aspects of his world will come between us just as my magic will. We're such different people - to share a life will present challenges no couple should have to overcome. I don't know if I'm brave enough to risk everything to have him. Hetty has said I must choose between my magic and James."

Esta made a most unladylike snort. "Hetty isn't all-knowing. She doesn't have a man to call her own, does she?"

Kat shook her head. Her sister didn't need to know about the countless men Hetty had shared her life with, all of whom died well before her. The old witch had experienced both sides of this. If she couldn't rely on Hetty for advice, she could rely on no one.

Esta took her hands and looked into her eyes. "Please don't throw this away. Think long and hard about your answer. I can't express how happy Sam has made me. I don't understand how you can doubt James." She fixed Kat with a challenging stare. "Perhaps you don't love him after all?"

Kat realized what her sister was doing, but she couldn't stop the flood of passion that rose like a wave. "When I'm with him we are one. When we're apart it's as though a piece of me is missing. I dream about him each night and all day which is why I've kept so busy. But it's not working!"

Esta pulled her close. "You do love James."

Kat shook her off. "I love him. That doesn't mean it's the right choice to marry."

"It's the right choice. You'll regret it if you don't."

Kat sighed. "I'll unpack and take a bath." She left before Esta could continue the conversation.

Kat climbed from the bath and wrapped a towel around her. She sat before the fire in her sitting room, toweling her long hair dry. The flames mesmerized her. They all meant well - her family. They wanted her to be as happy as they were. She wanted it too, but perhaps a man and a family weren't in the cards for her. James would find a wife and have children. The thought sent a sharp pang of jealousy through her. She had her hounds and her magic. There were causes she could fight. Solving the mystery of the dragon would be the first. The hounds could be her children. And there might be men along the way.

At the thought, James's face and body appeared in her mind's eye. He leant over her, speared her with his rod, and took her to paradise. Her belly tightened at the memory. She groaned. How could she manage the years ahead without him to slake her desire?

As Kat recalled the day in the wintery meadow, a face formed in the flames - an old, whiskery face.

"Hetty," she whispered. "How are you?" Her first fear was that her old friend was ill again.

"Fighting fit, girl. What of you? Still lifting your skirts for that man?"

Kat sucked in a breath. "I...no...I don't know."

"You sound like a young maid, not a woman in control of her own mind."

"Perhaps it's because I...oh, never mind. What's the news of Brightcastle?"

"Strange tidings indeed. It seems there might be a dragon tormenting these parts. I wondered if your hounds had told you anything."

Kat sighed. "I've seen the thing. It attacked James in Costa. He only just escaped with his life. The hounds knew it was coming, and I dreamed of it."

Hetty hissed and leaned closer. "Then it's true. I thought it might be the drunken ramblings of soldiers and guards."

"It's true. I intend to find it and discover what it wants."

"This makes what I have to say even more important." Hetty paused, and her image wavered as if her concentration faltered. Then she became clearer. "I'm handing my power and position to you, girl. My illness has shown me I'm vulnerable. I could've died, and all this knowledge stored in my head would've perished with me. Alecia can help, but she doesn't have the magic - the ability to be a powerful witch. You must come to me and step into my shoes. I'll guide you while I can."

Kat pulled her knees up to her chest and rested her forehead on them. Stacked on top of James's proposal and the heavy-handed advice of her family, this last ultimatum felt unfair. She was no child to be directed by those who thought they knew better.

"I don't know, Hetty," she said, raising her head. "I'm not ready to take on such a huge task." She didn't understand what it might entail. Her magic had always been about fighting, not focused on intrigue. "How do you foresee this occurring?"

"You must move to Brightcastle and live with me while you complete your training and become familiar with the skills you need to operate in my world. The duration of this training would be at least a year, and I assure you, by then, you'll be stronger than any witch I've ever encountered - including me." She fixed Kat with her unblinking stare, and it was as if Hetty sat in the same room. "You haven't encumbered yourself with that man, have you?"

Kat's hackles rose. Who the hell did Hetty think she was? "I have not."

"Good. Then you should make plans to move as soon as possible. There's no time to lose."

Hetty didn't wait for an answer but ended the conversation by fading out of the fire. Kat blew a breath through her teeth. She toweled her hair with greater vigor to let off some of the steam built up by Hetty's ultimatum.

Leave her family and move to Brightcastle, indeed! Have you encumbered yourself with a man, indeed! And what if she had? What if she welcomed James into her life? Did it mean Hetty wouldn't want her, might refuse to teach her? Was Hetty's way the only way? Or could Kat map out her future, create her own destiny, her own plan that may be equally or perhaps more successful?

She thought of James and his determination to follow his own calling rather than the one set by his parents. Perhaps they weren't so different after all. Perhaps he might understand her predicament.

She dressed in her breeches and tunic and threw a light cloak around her shoulders. It had been days since she rode Demon, and it might be what she needed to clear the cobwebs from her cluttered mind.

Within minutes, her horse was saddled, and Kat rode west through the forest bordering her estate. Demon was frisky - no, downright charged - so she gave him his head, delighted to have the wind in her face. They galloped along their favorite paths until the horse was a lather of foamy sweat over his neck and shoulders. She reined him in and walked him along the track until he stopped blowing. She kept the horse at a walk to prevent him getting cold and sore, but watched the trees to either side.

Soon she saw shapes moving through the forest and realized her hounds kept her company. She climbed a path then veered to the left off the main track and arrived at the top of a small hill that jutted from the forest canopy, allowing her a glorious view of the forest and the Aranati estate to the east. The forest trees were dotted with the russet tones of autumn. If she squinted, she could see the ocean. She loved this land, this kingdom.

The hounds surrounded her, as much a part of the land as she was, perhaps more. She had no idea where they came from, but they were now essential to her and she to them. They might make the difference between keeping the kingdom or losing it to the enemy – the *Sis Lenweri*. Or perhaps it wasn't even about the elves in the long run, but between the forces of magic, or even against magic as the king seemed to think.

She dismounted and the hounds drew close. She placed her palm on the forehead of each. Feelings and images came to her - long runs through the grass and forest, savage teeth in hare and deer, rutting, the dragon, and a large black she-dog that somehow, she understood was her. She longed to run with the hounds, but she could only do so in her dreams. It would have to be enough.

Then she had an idea. Let *them* be her guide. Image by image, she constructed scenes in her mind of Brightcastle and Hetty. The old witch seemed to spook several of the hounds. She showed them the streets and buildings, Hetty's house and kitchen, the palace and the people she knew in the town. She built more images of the trek to Brightcastle and what her life might be like if she lived there. Most of the beasts sat, their tongues lolling out, but the leaders growled and snapped at the air. Did it mean they wouldn't come with her?

She placed her forehead to these leader hounds and again read their thoughts. Dead and dying hounds lay in the streets, soldiers on horseback stabbing them repeatedly. The sharp metal pierced Kat again and again, and she wrenched herself away, her gut sick with the shared pain.

Was that what might become of her hounds if she followed Hetty's plan? Were they attempting to tell her they could die if she undertook the move? Night hounds were fighters, hunters. They must be ready to die, but she didn't wish to cause them more suffering. And if she chose to move to uproot her life, to sacrifice her chance at family life, she must also accept the cost, for herself, James, her family and her hounds.

James had made his choice to spy for the king. Were they even on the same side? Or was it murkier than one side or another? Her head whirled with choices and possible consequences. One thing was certain. This decision of hers - to fall in with Hetty's plan or accept James's proposal - was a crossroads, a defining moment. Kat was sure, if she made the wrong choice, there would be disaster, not only for herself but for her hounds and the kingdom.

She mounted Demon and made her way home, escorted by the hounds she had once feared.

CHAPTER 20

KAT needed no one's help to make the biggest decision of her life. They all tried, of course, except for Hetty, who seemed to believe, since she had delivered her ultimatum, all she must do was to sit back and wait for Kat to arrive on her doorstep.

She was the only one who hadn't tried to speak with her over the past two days. Her mother, sister, and brother-in-law all cornered her at various times. Esta had a habit of popping up when least expected, and found Kat even though she had a young child to keep track of. Kat had taken to mucking out the stable and completing tasks in the most far flung corners of the estate.

She bolted her dinner, spent the evenings in her room, then rose early and breakfasted before the others were up. She had become so jumpy she felt like one of her hounds.

Her dreams were full of the hounds, as if they had invaded her subconscious. Most of them were nightmares where all her beloved beasts were speared to death by armored soldiers. During the day, she couldn't stop yawning and snapped at anyone who came near. She kept drifting off, her thoughts turning to all her encounters with James, especially those where he had pleasured her. She lay in bed before sleep claimed her, touching herself to relieve the desperate desire she felt for him. No matter how hard she tried, her body waited for James, and no false loving would do.

After two days, she was desperate to escape. And so, she packed her saddle bags and set out for Costa. She would find him and settle this once and for all.

That evening, she arrived at his manor house on dusk. The housekeeper told her James was not at home. Kat was overwhelmed by a desperation she'd been fighting all day.

"I must see him, Mistress Lary."

"Then you must find him, Lady Katrine. But let me tell you this. I care for Master Tomel as if he were my son, and if you won't give him what he needs then get up on your horse and ride back to your home." She closed the door in her face.

Kat stood, shocked at those words. How dare his housekeeper take her to task when it was James who had ruined everything? She had been ready to give herself to this man who made her body sing, and *he* spurned *her*. Did Mistress Lary know that? *Of course not!*

She turned and mounted Demon, determined to do as James's housekeeper suggested - ride back home. She let Demon amble back the way they had come and was almost at the town wall when she reined him in. *What am I doing? I must see James.*

Kat turned her horse and searched Costa, beginning with James's jewelry shop. She shivered as she recalled her first visit to the shop and their battle with the night hound. Had it all been a test? Had the hounds been waiting for a worthy person to lead them? If so, it appeared she had passed their initiation. The shop was locked up tight. He wasn't in any of the other shops either.

Next, she patrolled the inns and taverns, gathering more unwelcome interest from patrons as she moved from the more respectable to the seedy end of town. James was not to be found and desperation seized her. Was he even in Costa? His housekeeper would have told her if James was away. Or perhaps not. Had she missed her chance to be with him? A tiny piece of her worried she might never see him again, though his actions demonstrated he wanted a life with her.

It was growing dark. Soon it would be dangerous to be out and about. She had no wish to expose her magic or fight for her life. The only lit building near her was the temple. It drew her like a moth to the flame. A prayer to the Goddess wouldn't hurt.

She tied Demon around the side of the building out of the wind and paused on the threshold. Taking a deep breath, she stepped inside. Her whole body trembled, and she drew her cloak around her. She tried to soak in the peace of the sanctuary, but the day had been too long and fraught. A man stood near the front where the candles burned as tribute to the Goddess. He had just placed a lit candle on the shelf. Her foot scraped on the step.

* * *

James turned as the sound of a footfall disturbed his prayer. Just his luck that even this small moment of peace should be denied him. A woman stood in the entry, seemingly poised for flight. Their eyes met. *Katrine.*

He dared not speak or move for fear he might scare her like the wild animal she resembled. Her eyes glittered, swirled, and sparkled. Suddenly, glowing red eyes flanked her.

"Katrine," he said. "Your hounds."

She sent the beasts into the night with a wave of her hand then turned back to him. It seemed some of her wildness had subsided. She took a step forward, then another.

"I thought I'd never find you," she said.

His heart leaped for joy. "You were looking for me?"

"I find myself at a crossroads," she said, her voice guarded. "I needed to speak to you before I could move on."

Was she here to say goodbye? "I won't let you leave without a fight."

Her eyes flared, reflecting the candlelight. "You want me still?"

James chanced a step forward. "I thought the ring would have spoken eloquently of my desire to have you in my life. I love you, Katrine."

He took another step, and she held up her hand to make him stop.

"I am yet to decide," she said, "but I can't get you out of my life, out of my head." "Perhaps there's a reason. Perhaps we're meant to be together."

She looked down at her boots, and, when she looked back up, her eyes had lost a little of their life. "Once I would've given anything to hear you say those words, to receive your ring and your promises. Indeed, I gave you something precious."

"I don't know what came over me that day. I allowed my body to rule, but I can't regret what happened, not honestly."

She turned to leave, but he grasped her hand. "Stay and hear me out." She didn't turn, so he spoke his words to her profile, the silhouette he loved; the brave, brash, and most alive woman he had ever met.

He took a deep breath, praying he could find the right words. "I regret not saving that moment for another day. Giving in to my desires was wrong. I can never truly make you believe I didn't intend to use you. But I'll try." He took another long breath, but she still refused to look at him. "I love you, Katrine Aranati. It has taken me months to accept my feelings for you. Now I understand I can't live without you. I've tried and failed. The day in that snowy meadow is one I'll never forget. The Goddess knows I tried to put you out of my head and out of my heart. I could not. The intensity of my feelings terrified me. I had tried so hard to control my destiny. I thought I had it all planned out."

She turned to him and tears shimmered in her blue eyes.

"And then you came along," he said, "and my heart took over. My body betrayed me, and I acted without regard for you and your reputation. But now I realize I love you, I can't be sorry I was your first. I've lain with no one else since. You ruined me for all other women, and I'm glad. You may not need me anymore, there may be many hurdles for us to jump, life may often be difficult. But I can't live without you. Please put me out of my misery and do me the honor of becoming my wife."

He dropped to one knee and looked up at the only woman he would ever want, could ever want. Might she put aside the hurt he had delivered her and agree to love him forever?

Katrine grasped both his hands. James closed his eyes to gather courage before fixing his gaze on hers.

"I'm not the girl you took in the meadow, James, and will never be that girl again. Too much has happened - the hounds, my dreams, Hetty—" She swallowed and started again. "Hetty has asked me to move to Brightcastle and take over from her. She's too old to continue her work. I'm considering her request, though it was more an order."

"And what's your decision?"

"I'm yet to choose. But back to us. It broke my heart the day I saw your wedding banns posted. You can't imagine how angry and hurt I was. Not only had you left me, but all the time you were committed to another. I had no concern for my safety and that enabled me to control the hounds because I had lost all fear of them. Losing you was devastating at the time, but now I realize it was all part of my coming into power. No doubt there will be other days when I must rise like a phoenix from the ashes."

James couldn't decide where this was going. She sounded so strong, so capable of living without him. *Goddess, please let her have mercy on me!* She pulled a chain from her bosom and lifted it over her head. Upon it was threaded the ring he'd given her. As he watched her remove the ring from the chain, a cold hand gripped his heart. Time slowed as he waited for her to walk out of his life forever.

"Hetty's ultimatum made me examine what the future might hold for me if I take the path of the sorceress."

She handed the ring to him, forced him to fold his fingers around it. His world shrank to the cold metal in his palm. He thought he had prepared himself for her rejection, but this moment proved he had not. He couldn't look at her as she drew breath to continue.

"I don't want Hetty's life. I want to be a wife and mother. I want to dwell in the bosom of my family. And the only man I wish to have by my side is you."

It was only then that he looked into her eyes. What he saw there told him she truly wanted him. He stood and threw his arms around her, crushing her to him.

"Yes, James, I say 'yes' to becoming your wife!"

"You're more than I've ever wished for. I'll love you and treasure you all our days. You'll never be sorry you said 'yes'." He reached for her hand, slid the ring onto her finger and covered her hands with his

She stepped back. "We still have much to decide. Somehow, we must fit your life with mine, for I won't give up my magic. I want children, and I want to help my kingdom as well. I'll track down the dragon and find those responsible for it. And I won't hide away like Hetty does, a spider spinning her web from the shadows."

His heart swelled with pride at this fierce woman who had agreed to be his. He pulled her close again, and her arms crept inside his cloak. They stood in the center of the temple, amidst candles signifying tribute and hope, a beacon of light in the darkness.

"I love you, Katrine, and you shall have all you desire and more. Together we'll fight the evil in this kingdom. Never fear I'll deny you again. I've thrown off the fear of old and am ready to adore you for the rest of my life."

She beamed up at him. "I've loved you since the first day when I almost galloped over you, I think. You've set me free of my melancholy and shown me the way forward. I know there will be strife between us, but there's so much love."

"And desire," James growled, nibbling his way down her neck until she trembled in his arms.

"I want you, James," she whispered against his throat.

He kissed her, savoring the sweet softness of her lips and the promise of her ripe body. "I vowed I wouldn't take you again until we were married," he said. "I was here tonight, praying you might find me. I realized the only way for me to have you was for you to come to me. And here you are." He kissed her again. "We'll find a priestess and be married this night, and I can spend the rest of my life making up for breaking your heart."

"You're forgiven, beloved," she said. "But if we don't find a priestess soon, I fear I'll make you break that vow."

He laughed and dragged her toward the back of the temple.

EPILOGUE

THEY were married that evening in the Temple of the Goddess in Costa, with only three priestesses for witnesses. Kat wouldn't have it any other way. A hundred candles lit the space as she pledged her life to James, and he promised to love and care for her until death parted them.

A joy she never imagined filled her heart, and the last of her doubts vanished as he kissed her. The celebrants drifted away after the final blessing, and they were alone at last.

"Come, My Lady," he said. "Your horse awaits."

Demon snorted as James helped her up, then sat behind her for the short ride back to his mansion. He carried her over the threshold and straight to his room where he kicked the door shut and laid her on the bed.

"I hope you're ready for a night of passion, my love," he said. "We'll sleep tomorrow."

And that was the theme of their nights for the next week. Make love all night and sleep all day. Kat was becoming a nocturnal creature, and her hounds weren't happy. However, James said it was their honeymoon and theirs alone. The world could wait. He turned all visitors away, and they made plans to travel to her family estate to celebrate their union properly.

Their mode of travel was the pony and cart - a much more intimate journey than it would have been on horseback. Eight days after their marriage, Kat arrived back in the bosom of her family. Esta's tears knew no end, and her mother wasn't far behind. Sam clapped James on the back as if he was glad to have another brother. Everyone was happy to see them united, and Kat secretly hoped she might be with child before the month was out. She cherished the idea she might already have James's son or daughter within her womb.

The only black cloud on the horizon was Hetty. Kat had yet to tell her mentor of her decision. After a week back on the estate, she could put it off no longer. She retreated to her room one night when James and Sam were sharing a cigar in the drawing room.

Tension tightened her gut as she waited before the fire. "Hetty, we must speak." She waved her hand before the flames, and the seamed face of the old witch appeared.

"Hello, child. You took a long time to return with your answer. It must be two weeks!"

She forced herself to maintain eye contact. "A little more than that. How are you, Hetty?"

"I'm well, but I don't have time to sit here chatting. Give me your answer, girl!"

Kat restrained the angry words that gathered on her tongue. She was a grown woman, not a girl, and she had every right to follow her own path without fear of upsetting Hetty.

"I'm sorry, but I've decided not to move to Brightcastle. I'll fight my fight here or wherever necessary, with James by my side." There! It was out in the open! Silence greeted her words.

"Hetty?"

"I'm here, child."

Was it her imagination or did Hetty's voice sound incredibly weary?

"It wasn't a decision I took lightly, and I'm grateful you asked me to take your place. But James proposed, and I said 'yes'."

"Love will come and go, but the work of keeping the kingdom safe will continue."

"There's no point in further discussion. I'll help you whenever I can, but James has to come first."

The face in the fire would've terrified most people. Kat's toes curled with regret.

"I'm sorry, Hetty. Please keep in touch."

Hetty's image faded from the flames, and Kat choked back a sob. Her old friend hadn't even wished her happy.

She paced back and forth across the rug, examining her dilemma from every angle. Could she keep Hetty content without risk to herself or James? It wasn't as if she'd refused to help her old friend, only ruled out moving to Brightcastle. Surely if she kept in touch through the flames, Hetty could summon her when needed? James must visit the city on a regular basis, and Kat would accompany him. She could learn what she needed over time and perhaps take up the mantle further down the track. Would her plan suffice to keep Hetty content and the kingdom safe?

James stepped into the room, and she immediately went to him, burying her face in his chest.

His strong arms engulfed her, and she felt better, more able to cope with whatever life might throw at her. If she ever worried about her decision to marry James, moments like this reinforced the fact she had chosen well. He was a joy and a comfort, and so many other things. Her face heated at the thought.

"What's the matter?" he asked.

She sighed, contentment seeping over the unrest of a moment before. "I told Hetty my decision. She wasn't happy."

"It's not your fault, Kat. She can't have her way in all things."

"She's trying to protect the kingdom and her magical heritage. I'm merely looking after myself."

He raised her face to his with one finger under her chin. "And what if we have children? Your magical abilities may be passed on. Isn't that important too?"

Kat took a deep breath as she imagined their dark-haired children, some of whom might cast spells in future. "You're right. Our children can be a force for good in the kingdom. I hadn't imagined that."

"Isn't there a way you can help Hetty without uprooting your whole world, or doesn't she want you under those conditions?"

Kat sighed. "I'm not sure. She was gone too quickly for me to ask. From my perspective, it's very possible for me to keep in touch and help when needed."

He hauled her against him. "Then that's what we'll do. We can visit Brightcastle whenever necessary, at least every few months. I need to take Princess Benae's tiara to her soon, so you'll accompany me. We'll sort it all out with Hetty."

"You would go with me?" Her heart bounded at the thought of confronting Hetty face to face. If she had James's solid presence at her side, perhaps she could approach her friend with certainty that her decision was the correct one. It was important Hetty understood they were a team.

"You know I will," he said, framing her face with his hands. "From now on, you and I will face everything together, the good and the bad, the joy and the sadness."

He lowered his lips to hers, and, in his embrace, Kat finally believed she was where she was meant to be.

THE END

GLOSSARY

Places

Kingdom of Thorius- the kingdom of men which encompasses the king's seat of Wildecoast and the prince's seat of Brightcastle

Wildecoast- city perched on the top of a cliff overlooking the sea on the east coast of Thorius; climate is mild but windy

Costa- coastal town around two days ride south of Wildecoast

Crystal Cave- a cavern on one of the Pinnacle islands, which lie off the coast south of Costa; it was the site of a treasure hunt but when Katrine broke through the magic protection, no treasure was found except one opal ear ring; she was almost killed disarming the magic trap

Brightcastle- large inland town surrounded by forests, around four days ride west of Wildecoast

People

Lenweri- the elven people who are tall and elegant with black skin and pointed ears; live in mountainous forests north and west of Thorius; also known as dark elves

Sis Lenweri- the faction of dark elves that wishes to take the kingdom of Thorius back from men

Defender- a race of shapeshifters who are created to defend those in danger; they sense those in need of their help; a Defender can shift into animal form and the ability is inherited through family lines

Characters

Katrine Aranati (Kat-reen Ar- an- arti) – sorceress and younger daughter of an impoverished farming estate south of Wildecoast; older sister is Esta Aranati; once a smuggler called Lady Star; heroine of **The Master and the Sorceress**

James Tomel (James Tom-elle)– master jeweler and oldest son of a farming family; lives in Costa; hero of **The Master and the Sorceress**

Esta Aranati- Katrine Aranati's older sister; she is head of the Aranati estate and was once a smuggler known as Lady Moonlight; heroine of **The Lady and the Pirate**

Samael Delacost - once a pirate, was captured by Nikolas Cosara, admiral of the King's Navy and is now sworn to obey the admiral or spend the rest of his life in prison; hero of **The Lady and the Pirate** and now married to Esta Aranati

Mistress Lary – James's housekeeper in Costa

Eva - James's maid in Costa

Dant – James's stable hand; has odd colored eyes, one blue and one green.

Lady Melanis Stenmore (Mel-arn-ee Stenmore) – attractive blonde noblewoman from Brightcastle; she is a wealthy young widow

Master Cal Delcore – master goldsmith in Brightcastle and friend of James

Princess Alecia Zialni- the king's niece and daughter of Prince Jiseve Zialni who once ruled in Brightcastle and was next in line to the throne

Vard Anton- the love of Princess Alecia's life and a shapeshifting Defender

Nikolas Cosara- admiral of the King's Navy; hero of The Lord and the Mermaid; half-brother to Samael Delacost- they share a mother, Vitavia

Reid Vetta- Master goldsmith in Wildecoast; once engaged to Esta Aranati; best friend of James Tomel

Master Anza- the master jeweler in Wildecoast to whom James was apprenticed

Queen Adriana- wife of the King in Wildecoast; is a patron of James Tomel

Night hounds- a beast the size of a wolf, with short grey hair, heavy snout, and stumpy ears; the eyes are red; there are six toes on each paw and the back feet have retractable cat-like claws, huge and razor sharp; have not been seen in Thorius for at least fifty years

About the Author

BERNADETTE Rowley is a lover of epic fantasy who is a veterinarian by day and an author by night. She is currently published in the genre of fantasy/paranormal romance with six books, all set in her fantasy world of Thorius.

When she was a young teenager, an aunt gave her a copy of The Sword of Shannara by Terry Brooks and Bernadette has lived in various fantasy worlds ever since. So it's no surprise that her chosen genre when writing romance is fantasy.

"I can see these settings so vibrantly in my mind and hope my readers can too."

But Bernadette has no desire to spoon-feed her readers by laboriously describing her fantasy settings. She would rather the reader use their own imagination a little.

Along with sword and sorcery, dashing heroes and stunning heroines, this author includes strong healing themes in many of her books- an element which is central to her everyday job. "When I started writing this series, I never imagined my day job would force its way into my stories as it has."

And, of course, there are animals, especially Bernadette's beloved horses, as well.

Bernadette lives in Brisbane, Australia, with the four heroes in her life- her husband Michael and three grown sons.

Connect with the Author

Website: www.bernadetterowley.com
Subscribe to the Bernadette Rowley newsletter and
get a free map of the world of Thorius

Facebook: www.facebook.com/bernadetterowleyfantasy
Twitter: www.twitter.com/bt_rowley